ZANE PRESENTS

THE AWAKENING

Book I

THE CHRONICLES OF THE NUBIAN UNDERWORLD

Dear Reader:

Wow! All I can say is get ready for a wild ride as Shakir Rashaan takes you into the BDSM lifestyle. His narrative is so real that it's obvious he's a true practitioner and has been for fifteen years in Atlanta's African-American Fetish community.

His erotica is off the chain, one of the reasons I selected his story for *Zane Presents Z-Rated: Chocolate Flava 3.* The talented writer brings it raw.

In *The Awakening*, Book One of *Chronicles of the Nubian Underworld*, Shakir introduces us to Ramesses and his wife, Neferterri, and their submissives. Discover what goes on at The Palace led by Amenhotep, Ramesses' mentor, stays there, and what goes on is some of the freakiest erotica on the planet. Book One centers around Amenhotep's welcoming his newest slave.

The tale highlights the acts in this spicy world as readers venture to the "dark side" with twists to keep you eager to complete the journey.

The story is written in true style with the dominants referred to in uppercase and the submissives in lowercase.

Be sure to check out Shakir's next titles in the series, *Legacy* and *Tempest*.

As always, thanks for supporting myself and the Strebor Books family. We strive to bring you the most cutting-edge, out-of-the-box material on the market. You can find out about our other authors on www.zanestore.com and you can find me on Facebook @AuthorZane and on Twitter @planetzane. Or you can email me at zane@eroticanoir.com.

Blessings,

Zane

Publisher
Strebor Books
www.simonandschuster.com

"It's exhilarating to be alive in a time of awakening consciousness; it can also be confusing, disorienting, and painful."

—*Adrienne Rich*

ZANE PRESENTS

A NOVEL

SHAKIR RASHAAN

SBI
STREBOR BOOKS
NEW YORK LONDON TORONTO SYDNEY

Strebor Books
P.O. Box 6505
Largo, MD 20792
http://www.streborbooks.com

This book is a work of fiction. Names, characters, places and incidents are products of the author's imagination or are used fictitiously. Any resemblance to actual events or locales or persons, living or dead, is entirely coincidental.

ISBN 978-1-59309-544-4
ISBN 978-1-4767-4872-6 (ebook)
LCCN 2013948766

First Strebor Books trade paperback edition December 2013

Cover design: www.mariondesigns.com
Cover photograph: © Keith Saunders/Marion Designs

10 9 8 7 6 5 4 3 2 1

Manufactured in the United States of America

To my Beloved,
Through the storms
Through the fire
It has only made our bond stronger
I love you

ACKNOWLEDGMENTS

Okay, first things first, before you read this particular book. This is (somewhat) a work of fiction. That means that some of this stuff was made up, and some of it includes players whose names have been changed to protect the (not so) innocent.

I wanted to bring things along at a slow burn, so to speak, when I first envisioned the *Nubian Underworld* series, to kind of give folks a way to slowly take a peek and see if they liked how things developed. It is my sincerest hope that I accomplished what I set out to do, and that you're willing to delve deeper into the Underworld with me.

Before you even dig into this first installment, I'm already finished with the next *Nubian Underworld* installment, *Legacy*. I'm putting something a little outside-the-box out there, sort of a pipe dream that I would implement if I ever won the lottery. Not just a couple million though, I mean BIG money. I'm really excited to see how that idea might play out. I'm also thinking that a few people, possibly even a couple of submissives, might get a voice that didn't get one in the first book. You never know, you know?

I know there might be some folks that will read this book and might think, "That type of stuff doesn't happen. Black folks don't do stuff like that." Guess what? Truth can be stranger than fiction sometimes...and I'm gonna leave it at that for now.

Some things in the book actually happened, and some stuff was made up. Wait, I think I said that somewhere in this part already. Oh well, it's up to you as to what's real and what's been made up.

Yeah…like I'm really gonna tell which is which. SMH.

I'm really starting to dig this whole "literary universe" thing. I think I'll call mine the "NEBU Universe," just because I want to have a flair for the dramatic. LOL. Hopefully, if enough of an audience is established, I'll be able to branch out a bit and do some other stuff. Perhaps even do some vanilla books? Nah, that's too predictable.

I want to first thank the Almighty for allowing me the ability to put this novel together.

Don't you just love it when people do that?

Seriously, I do understand why, because it takes a lot of work, time, sacrifice and a little luck to be able to have everything come together as well as you can put it together.

I've probably thanked damn near everyone that could be in the last couple of years, but it bears repeating sometimes because without their love and support, I wouldn't be able to do what I do.

To my mom: thank you, thank you, thank you for all of the love and support, not only of my lifestyle choices, but actually taking the leap of faith and realizing that it wasn't as bad as you thought it was. I am blessed to have you, and everything that I do, and have ever done or tried to do, has been to make you proud. I hope this novel continues to do just that.

To my sister: I know I could have told you sooner about a lot of things, but better late than never, right? LOL. Thank you for understanding the things that I've done and the connections that I have and the reasons for them. I know it's not exactly traditional, but it's stood the test of time, and God willing, it will continue to do so. I'm glad that I was able to inspire you to take the plunge with me with this writing thing, and I'm excited as hell to see what you come up with next!

To my Beloved: there are never enough words to express the love that I have for you. You are without a doubt the best I will ever have, and to take this life's journey with you, I couldn't have asked for anyone else. As we've always said, "United in battle, until death do we part."

To my father: a lot of what I am as a man, I took a part from you and made it my own, with my own swagger on top of that. We may not have seen eye to eye on a lot of things, but you have always allowed me to be my own man, and for that I will be forever grateful.

To my Nana and Granddaddy: even though you're no longer here, I take comfort in the fact that you're sitting pretty, together, watching your eldest grandchild do his thing on his terms.

To my son and daughter: I know you both were wondering what daddy was up to late at night, and I know I've told you both that you couldn't read what I was coming up with, but know that I wasn't saying things just to be saying them, and one day you'll understand why (like, when you turn twenty-one and I won't CARE what you're reading. LOL).

To our extended Leather Family (yes, I'm only using your scene names): Sir Deme and solamente; AMP Sir EZ; my mentor and big brother, Master Obsidian, and his wife, namaste; my Beloved's mentor, Master Black Zeus; finally, Lady D and Lady Velvet G. Thank you all for your support when I first started cranking up this book writing thing. We don't call a lot of people in the BDSM community as a whole "Family" often, but we consider you as such. Thank you for letting me pick your collective brains to bring all of these characters to life.

To our submissive girls, aneesa and ayanna, who influenced a lot of the behavior of the submissives and slaves in this series, thank you both. You know I appreciated the answers to my maddening questions.

To my SoCal crew: Sir Strange, Orpheus Black and the rest of y'all, we're hoping to finally get out there and getting some fun and sun soon! To my DMV crew: Mythos3K, kore3K, Lady Z, amara and the rest of y'all up there, thanks for all of your support! MrCL and MsSquirt, destny and the rest of the folks in NYC, and last but not least, my crew here in the A: hypnotiq, Jupiter and Skyy, Trinity; man, it's so many of y'all down here, just know I'm including you, too

LOL!

I know I'm missing a whole gang of folks, so just do me a favor and insert your name in this next statement:

I'd like to thank ______________________________ for the support and love. I hope to continue to put books out that you will want to tell your friends and family about.

Anyway, let me get back to trying to come up with some twisted stuff to put in print that people think POC (I'm sorry, that means people of color, or black people in particular, folks) can't get into… and don't forget to tell a friend or two, or a hundred; you never know who might get a kick out of reading this. A bruh would like to make a few bestseller lists. LOL.

Sincerely,

Shakir Rashaan

SPECIAL NOTE TO READERS

The grammatical errors that you might see within the dialog between the characters are not oversights. This is the type of speech and text that is used in some facets of the BDSM world. As one of my submissive friends put it, "The lowercase letters in a slave's or submissive's name are a demonstration of the hierarchical relationship. It is a reminder to the submissive that he or she is the bottom part of the hierarchy, meant to be led, and the Dominant's name is always capitalized, as He or She is the Top part, meant to lead." In keeping with the essence of the series and the essence of the BDSM community, preserving the speech was paramount. It is my hope that you, the reader, will understand and appreciate the symbolism.

INTRODUCTION

Welcome to the Chronicles of the Nubian Underworld: a view into our world of the alternative, and the circle of friends within this realm that my Beloved and I associate with. We hope you enjoy the journey with us as you come to meet up with some of the friends and associates, as well as some new faces, which will come about through this first of a hopefully long series of "Chronicles" yet to come.

Now, I think I know what you might be thinking, but here's the real: this is a lifestyle. Everyone has a little freak in them, but the difference is we have found like-minded people who don't judge. They just enjoy themselves and the friendships that are made within the lifestyle community, and the freedom of being within that community.

Oh, I'm sorry, forgive my manners; I forgot to introduce myself. Depending on the community that you happen to meet us in, our names are separate within each world. If at a swingers' nightclub, you can call me Kane, and my wife's name is Mercedes. We have a few memberships at a couple of these clubs, but we don't attend them often, mainly because it's not really our style when it comes to swingers' clubs. Not that we don't enjoy ourselves there when we do go, but we have a different belief system than some of the "New Age" swinging couples that are out there. But that's another story for another time. So, for the most part, you can refer to us by those names when we're within the vanilla world.

If at a dungeon or a BD/SM club or munch, then you may refer to me as Lord Ramesses, and my wife's name is Lady Neferterri. The girls that I mentioned earlier are nicknamed shamise, jamii, and nuru, and are our submissive girls within Our D/s "House," which we have given the name of Kemet-Ka, roughly translated from the Egyptian meaning of "the essence of Egypt." My wife and I consider ourselves that rare breed of "libertines" who enjoy the variously different aspects of the alternative lifestyle, as well as the people within each of them.

Now, I'm sure it may confuse some of you when you see us switch roles and names throughout, but it is a necessary evil, so to speak. You simply cannot use the same names because they don't always have the same meanings within each realm. After a while, you get used to it, and almost come to expect it. Such is the way of things.

Regardless of what you've read or seen on HBO, we are ordinary people. We go to work; some of us even own businesses. We pay taxes, and a lot of us are very spiritual people. We are in very stable relationships, even married for long periods of time. We raise families, and our children are very stable. The thing that separates us from "normal" people is we enjoy doing more than just two positions while making love.

Oh, and one more thing: we do this in the privacy of our homes, so it's none of your business what we do, unless we make it your business. But enough of me chatting; we're gonna be late.

1 RAMESSES

"Baby, we're going to be late for the party." I heard my wife, Neferterri, calling from upstairs. "You know how Amenhotep is about beginning His ceremonies before we get there."

I was in the basement of our house, loading up the bags we would need for our night at Master Amenhotep's estate. Tonight was special indeed as Amenhotep was inviting the community to witness the collaring ceremony of His newest slave, safi. She was the latest of the slaves who reside with Him in Palmetto on the south side of Atlanta.

"I'm almost done, babe. Have either of the girls gotten here yet?" I asked out loud.

"shamise is here with Me now, helping Me with My corset. jamii and nuru should be here any minute," Neferterri replied.

It was almost ten o' clock, and usually our submissive girls are on time. Since it was a busy weekend in Atlanta and they were coming from different directions to the house, I decided not to punish them unless they made us extremely late. Amenhotep's estate wasn't far from where we resided in Fairburn, but I had to make sure we were set up in our designated area in the dungeon before the ceremony began at midnight. He could care less if anyone else was late, but I already knew Amenhotep would have a fit if He had to start without me.

I finished up the last of the bags when I heard all three girls coming down the stairs, assuming their kneeling positions at my feet. "we're here, my Sir. May we take the bags to the car?" nuru asked as her eyes lowered.

"Yes, you may, girls. shamise, let your Goddess know we will be leaving soon." I kissed my girls on their foreheads as they each took a bag and headed back upstairs.

I took notice of each of the girls' attire, and I had to say, I couldn't have been a prouder Dominant as I took in their collective beauty.

shamise wore a strapless black corset, a gift from Neferterri and me last Christmas, and accentuated it with a wrap skirt draped slightly above her knees. I smiled at the way the skirt could be easily opened and available for access to do whatever I wanted. Knowing I had a fetish for heels, she didn't disappoint, but she took things a step further, wearing knee length, four-inch heeled boots. We named her shamise, which means "first born" in Arabic and Egyptian, because she's our "Alpha" submissive.

Her diamond collar was proudly adorned around her neck, displaying diamond handcuff earrings that dangled from her earlobes. To complete her look, she wore her hair up to expose her neck and show off her collar.

jamii wanted to be a bit more demure in her appearance than her sis, but surprised us in her choice to wear a miniskirt and a black leather halter top instead of hiding her legs with pants. She's not as much of an exhibitionist as our other two girls, usually choosing to wear a pant suit. She also decided on boots, wearing an ankle-length, four-inch stiletto style. We named her jamii, which means "sexy or sexually enticing" in Swahili, and she tried to live up to the meaning of her name tonight.

The slick smile on my face conveyed my appreciation of her new found confidence in her body and sexuality. The sharpness of her look was completed by her Chinese bob haircut, which showed off her own collar, presented to her in a private ceremony a little less than a year ago.

Finally, the "baby girl" of the House, nuru, wore a pleated school-girl skirt, a halter top, too, and four-inch "Mary Jane" heels with bobby socks, putting her hair up in pigtails and sucking on a lolly-pop. Because of her bubbly and happy personality, we gave her the name nuru, which means "brightness, or light" in Swahili.

Now, I feel I have to explain to those that might not be in the "know," so, indulge me for a quick moment. Alpha submissives within a Poly Household are usually the first to have been collared by their Dominant. They are responsible, in some cases, to train the submissives that are collared after them, making sure that their submissive sisters know the rules of the House as well. Beta submissives...well, they are as the moniker suggests, the second submissive to be collared within the House.

Considering my Beloved and I currently have three girls right now, we usually treat them equally, as to not play favorites, but within a House of this size, there are those times when we will defer to shamise over the other girls because she's been with us the longest.

Forgive me for the quick lesson, but I didn't want to confuse anyone. Let's get back to the story, shall we?

For a minute, I forgot we needed to attend a collaring ceremony.

I watched my Beloved walk down the stairs. The look in her eyes was evidence she wanted me to get a good look at her outfit for the evening.

"So, do You like, My Pharaoh?" Neferterri asked while doing a model's twirl in her strapless corset, complete with a ruffled petti-coat skirt, which showed off my wife's "ASSets" quite well.

I shook my head. I counted myself lucky to have such beautiful women in my life, including my daughters. Our oldest was thirteen, our middle child was eleven, and our youngest was eight. To be surrounded by such beauty, as the pharaohs of the Ancient Kingdom had done so long ago, was a sight to behold.

"Your Pharaoh likes this outfit very much, baby," I said, no longer resisting the urge to rub my hands over her hips and kiss my beautiful wife. "You look good enough to eat…damn."

Neferterri playfully slapped at my hands, putting up a small fight, finally giving in to the kisses being placed on her neck and shoulders. I started to lift the skirt to get a better grasp of her ass and try to take things to the next level for a quickie, but shamise unintentionally interrupted us while coming to retrieve the last of the toy bags.

"Oops, sorry, didn't mean to interrupt You." shamise blushed over seeing her Dominants in an intimate moment. It wasn't the first time she'd caught us in a compromising position, and under normal circumstances, she would have quietly watched until we were finished. However, she knew if she did this time around, we'd all be in some serious trouble. "Daddy, You said we were going to be late if we didn't get going now. We don't want to keep Master Amenhotep waiting."

She was right. The last thing I needed was to be reprimanded by my mentor. He was a stickler for starting grand events on time. So, we grudgingly headed upstairs to finish packing the cars to head down to our destination.

Amenhotep's estate, *The Palace*, was an extravagant fifteen-bedroom home He'd purchased from a former CEO of a Fortune 500 company. The house had it all, complete with a front driveway that stretched out a half mile from the main road, 300 acres of land for ultimate privacy, especially with the things that went on outside of the house, a spacious basement which housed a twenty-seat projection room among the other amenities in the dungeon, and a 300,000-gallon pool to boot. For a man who had nine slave girls, and was about to collar a tenth, that's still a lot of house to deal with. But Amenhotep didn't worry about such things. He had ten male service slaves who were sent out by their owners to tend to the estate on a weekly basis, and three of his slave girls were designated service slaves as well.

It was a lot larger than the four-bedroom, three-car garage home with basement Neferterri and I owned, but hey, we all had to start somewhere, right?

As we drove up to the front door, I noticed the way the lighting was set up for the special occasion: the "House" colors of Crimson and Black were on proud display, and could be seen from the specialized lighting surrounding the house before we even had a chance to turn into the driveway. The service "bois" were outside, as usual, parking the cars in the designated area as the guests arrived, with certain spots being held for *special* attendees, to mark their status within the community. These were usually the out-of-state guests who have national and international status within the BDSM community, as there would be some who were able to fly in for tonight's occasion. You would have thought a few dignitaries were in attendance tonight as well, as we saw the fleet of different limousines that were also parked in their area as well.

Neferterri and I had the same thought: this latest one must be something special for all of this to occur. But then again, knowing Amenhotep, it's always difficult to tell, as He was, Himself, nationally known and respected.

We were greeted at the front door by paka, Amenhotep's Alpha slave. She wore a black cigarette girl's outfit and four-inch heels. We all knew the rest of the girls would be specially outfitted tonight, and saw one of the other girls dressed in a see-through cat suit as proof. A new slave would be accepted among them, and it would be done in grand fashion, as each one of them had been acquired before her.

"Good evening, m'Lord, m'Lady. My Master has been expecting You." paka bowed her head as she spoke, in show of respect. "May this girl relieve You of Your submissives so they may prepare Your area and Your room?"

Neferterri answered, "Yes, you may, paka. They know what they need to do."

paka nodded as she led jamii and nuru to the dungeon area in the basement, while the other of the slave girls, jazi, led shamise up to the bedroom to unload the baggage.

"paka looks radiant tonight, don't You think?" Neferterri asked me as paka disappeared with our girls.

"You know she made sure she outshined the other girls, baby," I remarked, noticing the extra sway in paka's hips as she walked away from us. "You should know that everyone in the house knows where she stands, regardless of whose night it is."

"Well, I guess we need to find out who is in attendance, and where they all are," Neferterri commented, leading the way, grinning as she noticed the way I always enjoyed the view while following her.

We walked through the main foyer, passing by the other guest bedrooms on the main floor, noticing the new changes to the walls, including the paintings hung since our last visit a month ago. We dropped by the dining area to pick up some hors d'oeuvres, noticing the other slave girls going about their business during a function such as this one, catering to the VIP guests, making sure wine-glasses were kept full. I took notice of the risqué outfits the girls wore, and a mischievous grin spread across my lips. Having witnessed each of their collaring ceremonies, I knew what each of them was capable of doing behind closed doors.

Well, not exactly *closed* doors.

My Beloved slapped my forearm, shaking me out of my lustful thoughts. I grabbed my arm in mock protest, glaring at her as I felt the sting rushing through my arm. She didn't flinch an inch. "You better be glad I love You, or I would have smacked that grin off Your face."

I smirked, slipping into her personal space to brush my lips against hers. She tried to move away from me, but I held her in place, holding her gaze for a few seconds before kissing her deeply. I moved my hands to the small of her back as we lost ourselves in the embrace. Once I heard the contented moan escape her lips, I broke from the kiss, watching the look in her eyes and gaining a measure of satisfaction of my own.

"No matter what happens, no one comes between us, Beloved." I caressed her cheek as I pulled her hand to my lips to kiss it. "United in battle, until death do we part, remember?"

"I remember, Beloved." She kissed me again. "Now, let's head outside and see what's going on."

Once we made it out to the backyard and pool area, even we were a little wide-eyed at some of the activity:

Different sub bois, completely naked, serving their Dominas with Cheshire cat grins on their faces.

Topless submissive girls, wearing G-strings and thong bottoms… some with their collars on, their leashes in their mouths, in their kneeling position waiting for their Dom to collect them.

Some pony play being demonstrated in the pool itself, with some of the pony boys in full rigors, carrying their owners with pride.

Spankings in open spaces…

Floggers flying through the air, hitting their intended targets…

Needless to say, it's a good thing Amenhotep did have all this privacy. If a neighbor saw half of what was taking place in the pool, much less around the pool, He would have heard from the local police a long time ago.

A funny image of two officers coming to the door to follow up on a disturbance call came to my mind. That would have been an interesting quandary: would the officers do their duty and ask the crowd to disperse, or would they simply look at all the freakiness around them and tell the owner to "keep the noise down?"

I knew what I would have done, but I wasn't a cop.

After scanning around and viewing the activity around us, we finally noticed Amenhotep with safi at the edge of the pool in the gazebo. She looked quite content with her pink bikini top and sarong bottom caressing her olive skin like the fabric was made only for her. Amenhotep wouldn't have it any other way when it came to His girls. When He gave them His undivided attention, He made sure they felt it.

Once He made eye contact with us, He waved us over. We headed over to join them in the gazebo, greeting other guests briefly along the way.

"So, You finally decided to come on down," Amenhotep stated while stroking safi's hair. "I was about to collar this one without You, Ramesses."

Looking down at the lovely piece of beauty being happily stroked by her Master, I responded, "Now, I was there for paka and all the other girls. There was no way I would miss breaking in Your newest girl."

Neferterri happened to notice a slight smile spread across safi's face as we were speaking, and she asked, "Does that excite you, slave?"

safi looked up at her Master first to silently ask permission to answer, which was protocol within His House, and once Amenhotep nodded, she quietly replied, "Yes, m'Lady. All the other girls told me once I performed my scene with m'Lord, it would seal this girl's place in the house."

safi then crawled to the area where I stood, kneeled at the base of my feet, and humbly stated, "This girl hopes to be everything my Master has built me up to be, m'Lord."

safi trembled as I moved closer, her body language giving away a lot more than what her words conveyed to me. I inhaled the perfume radiating from her skin, surrounding and captivating my senses. Once again, my reputation preceded me, and I didn't need this one to have an anxiety attack before I touched her. Amenhotep had been speaking to His girls about tonight, I guessed, and the other slave girls do enjoy it when He allows them to scene with me, as ours enjoy their time with Him as well.

To reassure her, I kissed her forehead and whispered into her ear, "Amenhotep would never have placed you in front of Me if He didn't think you would make Him proud, little one."

safi relaxed a little, crawling back to her place at Amenhotep's feet to continue enjoying her rare private attention she got from Him.

"So, who else has decided to come out for this occasion? I see some guests from the Northeast have come down this time," Neferterri inquired, obviously noticing all of the new attendees around the pool. "I haven't seen this many newbies in one spot since we collared jamii last year."

Amenhotep stroked His beard, which was what He always did when He was in deep thought. "Let's see...I know Lord Magnus and His slave girl jewel are here from Philly, and I think Master Orion is also here from Miami, and Mistress Sinsual and Her boi tiger are here as well. Oh, Mistress Blaze is here somewhere with Her girls," He explained. "There are a few new Doms here from the West Coast as well. Master Altar, You remember Him from Dragon*Con®? Well, He will be performing the ritual tonight, and His slave girl is with Him also, chastity."

My eyebrow rose, mainly because something was amiss. It's not like Amenhotep to break protocol and tradition unless something really went wrong. "Yeah, I do remember Altar, ran into him at one of the dungeons out on the west side about a month ago. Cool dude. What happened to Master Cypher?"

"Damn, You mean no one told You?" Amenhotep shook His head. "Ol' Cypher got caught up in a sting at His house. Turns out, He had been breeding some girls, and one of them turned out to be sixteen. So sad, but He was stupid for doing it."

I was taken aback by the news, but I really didn't feel sorry for him. There was usually an honor code amongst the male Dominants in the community, *especially* Dominants of color, whether local or national, and frankly speaking, there are some things I simply believe are not honorable for a Dominant to do: abusing His property and using them for profit are at the top of my list. Breeding ranks up there with prostituting women, submissive or not. We had enough problems with people who wanted to understand what we enjoy and completely missing the point, not to mention the fakes out there confusing power exchange with being a control freak. But, oh well. That's the difference between the Leather veterans of the community, and these new wave nuts who think they can research on the Internet and instantly become a Dom or Master.

Yeah, I said it, and I dare anyone to tell me otherwise.

"Oh yeah, I almost forgot," Amenhotep added. "Some of Your swinger couples are also coming by. It seems they might actually want to stop playing around doing all the simple fucking and come to the dark side where they might want to explore some real things."

Now, that meant a few things. The couples he mentioned were Jay and Jasmine, who were new to the swing scene, but had been a part of our circle of friends for a long time.

As for Ice and Kitana...well, let's simply say these two were a case study in "what took so damn long?" They have been around us for the past three years, but they never really made the jump to participating in a dungeon atmosphere before now after being so curious about it for so long.

Finally, there was Candy and her new man of the month, although I had a feeling this dude wouldn't survive the night, either. They never did. Candy and Neferterri are best friends, and my "concubine," but I'll have to explain another time.

"Anyway, we'll break them in when they get here." I passed it off as second thought. "Where is Mistress Sinsual anyway, or do I already know the answer?"

Before I could answer, I felt arms moving around my waist and the greeting, "Hi, Daddy," coming from behind me.

Now, since our submissive girls were all tending to their tasks before the ceremony, and Neferterri was standing right beside me, it could only mean one woman was standing behind me.

"Have you forgotten who you're talking to, Candy?" I sternly asked. Bringing out my Dominant side when I was not already in that mindset was not something I tolerated, unless they were ready to deal with the consequences of their actions.

Candy wasn't having it. "Now You know that shit doesn't fly

with me. I belong to Your wife, remember?" She even had the nerve to stand there, hands on her hips, daring me to do something about it.

I was not about to have her trip out and get away with it, so, I promptly sat in a chair, pulled Candy over my knee, slid her skirt up over her ass exposing her mocha skin, and before I commenced spanking, I asked her again, "Have you forgotten your place, Candy, or do I need to remind you?" I didn't even care her date stood a few feet away from me. There were some things that had to be handled.

Candy heard the bass and extra volume in my voice and relented. "I belong to You, too, Daddy. I'm sorry; it won't happen again."

I still gave her a few good smacks on her bare ass cheeks to make sure that she understood that Daddy didn't play.

The crowd in the immediate vicinity stopped and turned in our direction, reacting like they'd heard a loud clap of thunder and wanted to see if a storm was coming. Leave it to me to draw crowds as usual, even with other spankings going on. Amenhotep raised His hand, alerting the spectators that there was nothing to see. He knew I wasn't going to kill her or anything, but what could I say? I drew crowds, and I could clear them as well, depending on the intensity of the thunderstorm.

"Forgive My brat, folks, she sometimes feels the need to act out when she misses Me." I calmed the crowd down, especially Jay and Jasmine, who had just arrived and saw the whole exchange. As long as they had known Candy, they'd never seen anyone handle her like that.

Amenhotep, shaking His head, answered my question, "Knowing Sin, She's already in the dungeon torturing some poor soul."

Neferterri, while trying to comfort Candy, laughed. Sinsual, being true to form, usually found more than a few willing newbies, mostly male submissives who want a taste of her flogging skills and knife play expertise.

"What poor soul?" Kitana asked, joining in on the conversation. She was still soaking wet from playing in the pool, and to be honest, the wet hair look combined with the bikini she wore made her look as sexy as she usually was completely dry. "Oh my Lord, Sinsual isn't at it again, is She?"

Even with what I did to Candy only a few minutes ago, I was being greedy, and a little bit mischievous, so I couldn't resist my reply. "I've told you about calling My name, Kitana. Do I need to put you over My knee so you can keep calling it?"

I didn't know if it was the liquor talking, or if she was once and for all tired of being teased, but Kitana's reply shocked everyone in the gazebo. "Please, Sir, I've been a bad girl. I didn't mean to call for You without Your permission. I need to be punished."

She chewed on her bottom lip, unsure if she'd said the right thing or made the right move. She got so shy it looked like she'd turned sixteen and was a virgin all over again, waiting on someone to deflower her and make her a woman. She wanted to make eye contact with me, but found herself unable to do so, letting her eyes focus on her trembling hands.

Needless to say, all eyes were on her.

Rather than respond to her comment in front of the folks in attendance, I shot Neferterri a quick look, grabbed Kitana by the hand and quickly led her to the first guest bedroom I could find that wasn't already occupied.

I needed answers.

2 ❧ RAMESSES

"Do you realize what you said out there?"

We sat in the bedroom as I tried to get a sense of what in the world had gotten into her. I sensed her apprehension, realizing she'd opened Pandora's Box with little understanding of the potential consequences of her actions. I needed to know without a shadow of a doubt that she knew what she'd done.

I looked deep into Kitana's eyes, the heat of her body resonating against me. The scent of her desires rose furiously to the surface, feeding the beast within, intoxicating me. I felt the answers coming, but I wasn't sure if I was really prepared for the truth of those answers.

"Yes, Sir, i do. i've been reading a lot on what You do with Your girls, You know, the whole D/s thing, and it's been turning me on… a lot." Kitana's eyes flashed as she spoke, and despite her inability to keep eye contact, she confirmed the questions in my mind: she *meant* every word she'd said earlier.

"Do you understand what you have been reading?" I inquired again. As a Dominant, I could not assume a power exchange unless I was sure the person in front of me was clear about what they were getting into.

"Yes, Sir, i do…at least, i think i do," Kitana replied. This time, she looked directly into my eyes as she spoke. Her eyes possessed a measure of confusion, pleading with me to ease the storm roiling within her being. "So, what happens now, Kane? I really, *really* want to do this, but I'm really scared and excited at the same time."

Now, for at least the past year, Kitana and I had been together sexually at swing parties we both happened to attend. She'd also been intimate with my wife before, so, she's not a complete stranger to us. In fact, she's damn near like family, she and Ice both. But the D/s realm was a completely different situation. Once a commitment was made, it was made for the duration of time that was agreed upon, whether it's for a week or a lifetime. It's more than "freaky sex thang," and Kitana had to be made to understand.

"First, if you're going to follow through, then you will address Me properly," I directed.

"Yes, my Lord," Kitana responded. I cast her eyes downward, to make her understand the application of the things she'd read about.

"Good girl. Second, you will make sure your husband knows and understands what is going on before you willingly submit to us." I stood from the bed to assert my power over her and then stepped closely enough to her so she could sense my presence.

"Do You mean, to You both, Sir?" Kitana initially queried, sounding confused over the way I expressed the terms of her submission. It was a response I was used to, as most POC, or people of color, in the D/s community were not exactly Poly.

"Yes, to Neferterri, too, young one," I clarified. "Is there a problem?"

As she replied, "No, Sir," I placed a hand on her shoulder. Despite the eighty-plus-degree weather outside, I surmised the reality of the situation was what caused her to tremble in front of me. I sensed something else, but I wanted verbal confirmation instead of assuming and making the wrong move.

"Is this turning you on now?" I asked.

"Yes...yes, Sir. i'm so wet right now, if You don't mind me saying so, my Lord." She picked up on my simple protocol pretty quickly, but she still had more to learn, as House protocol standards do become more intricate.

"I want you to be sure about this, Kitana, I mean, *really* sure." I kissed her cheek as

I spoke to her. "you mean the world to us, and I don't want things to get too complicated once you make your decision to be ours. This isn't the swinging you're used to; there's a little more depth to this, baby."

"Sir, i'm serious. i'm scared as hell of what i'm feeling, but i'm serious about seeing how deep this can go, if i can say so, Sir," Kitana retorted without hesitation. "i would like to submit myself to You and be considered as a submissive in Your House."

Neferterri found us in the bedroom, and she sensed something was definitely up.

Once she noticed Kitana's body language, a smile spread across her face.

"So, you are serious after all?" she asked Kitana.

Kitana looked to me for response, but I only shook my head. "you heard your Goddess, Kitana. Answer Her question."

"Yes, my Lady, i am very serious. i need to understand why this is turning me on so much," Kitana answered. "i'm hoping to learn all i can from You both."

"Then kneel before your Sir, little one," Neferterri commanded. "I will adjust your position once you do."

To our amazement, Kitana kneeled and assumed the same position the girls have learned and mastered. The only thing Neferterri had to do was adjust her legs so that they were spread properly.

"It's what I thought. She will make an excellent acquisition, Beloved," she mentioned, subconsciously licking her lips. "I didn't think she was quite yet ready, but with the proper training, she could be as good as the other girls."

"my Lady, may i speak?" Kitana waited until Neferterri answered her. "i want to make You proud of me, proud to show me off in public in the future. i assure You both i am very excited to begin my training. That is, if You are willing to have me?"

Neferterri knelt and gave Kitana a soft kiss across her lips. She wanted her to realize this wasn't a dream, but she didn't want to deprive her of the magic of the moment we shared.

"We care very deeply for you, Kitana, otherwise we wouldn't be considering this with you," Neferterri answered her. "If you're willing to go slowly with this, I believe you will become an excellent submissive within this House."

paka opened the door and quietly entered the room. "m'Lord, m'Lady, my Master is ready to begin the ceremony. my Master requests Your presence, Lord Ramesses."

"Thank you, paka, would you please inform your Master I will be there in five minutes?" I replied before she bowed in reverence and left the room.

Focusing my attention back to Kitana, I knelt beside her and commanded, "you will accompany your Goddess to our area in the grand room. There, you will place yourself with our girls and kneel so you may witness your first collaring ceremony. We will discuss your consideration period after tonight has concluded. Do you understand Me, little one?"

"Yes, my Lord, as You command," Kitana answered as she and Neferterri left the room.

I took a minute to compose myself now that I was alone with

my thoughts. This unexpectedly wonderful turn of events was beyond my wildest dreams, but I had to ensure the rest of the guests did not sense the excitement and, dare I say, giddiness that came with new relationship energy.

Yes, I thought to myself, *this will definitely be an interesting night after all.*

Only, I didn't know how interesting until I got to the grand room for the ceremony.

☥

Decadent…

That's the word I would use to describe the dungeon where safi's collaring ceremony would take place.

From the carpet on the floor, thick and plush to the touch of bare feet, to the weaponry and extensive collection of leather, suede, and horsehair floggers hung on the walls, the room looked as it had in the past when the sister submissives before safi enjoyed their respective ceremonies. The St. Andrews Cross was displayed in the center of the room. Leather cuffs adorned at the four posts, where the submissive of honor had her wrists and ankles bound. Beside the Cross a few feet away, a collaring ceremony kneeling bench, laced in gold and ruby stones, was awaiting its latest participant in such a glorious event.

I still suffered from the goose bumps and mild excitement brewing within me. After all, I had assisted in these ceremonies since He first collared paka over ten years ago. I was barely out of college when Amenhotep insisted I knew the ways of a proper collaring ceremony so I wouldn't screw it up when I collared my own submissives in time. No matter how many times I have been and will continue to be involved with collaring ceremonies, I swore the excitement and the anticipation never got old. It kept me on my toes at all times, to make sure I did not get the protocol wrong or skip any steps, either. I had a reputation to live up to, and I would not disappoint, not tonight, or any other night.

safi was dressed in next to nothing. It was Amenhotep's bidding to ensure nothing was hidden from His view while they were in His presence. She was kept barefoot on the carpet as her arms and legs were fastened to their appropriate spots on the St. Andrews Cross, and her preparation was completed with my fastening the blindfold over her eyes. With a nod from Amenhotep, I began the ceremonial flogging and whipping session with safi. I began using a variety of different pieces of equipment: the leather floggers, the cat-o-nine tails, a couple of pinwheels, and paddles, too.

safi had already earned a reputation as a pain slut, meaning the more pain she received, the more aroused she became, up to and including to the point of orgasm. I felt the heat from her skin as I continued the pace. I alternated the usage of different pieces on her lower back, legs, ass, taking care not to miss a single spot on her skin, yet avoid damaging any body parts. The crowd was in complete silence, leaving safi's moans and gasps of ecstasy to fill the room. They took notice of the art of the welts on her skin as I continued my session, taking breaks between switches to make sure safi had not taken off into subspace on me without my knowledge.

safi never once uttered her safeword, which pleased her new Master immensely. I kept wary of the time I spent for her session, making sure to leave enough energy for her final task. I finally removed the restraints from her wrists and ankles, eliciting the help of another Dominant to help keep her upright. The entire time, I kept up the communication in safi's ear, ensuring she was still in the room with us all. After taking her down from the Cross, I silently commanded her on all fours so she could crawl to her place at the ceremonial kneeling bench and to assume a special kneeling position to recite her pledge.

Master Altar stood with Amenhotep in front of the crowd. safi knelt proudly, displaying the marks of her ceremonial session with me. As the specialized diamond-encrusted collar that prominently displayed "safi" across the front was placed and clasped around her neck by Altar, the crowd applauded. A subtle hand gesture from Altar quieted the applause as all eyes focused on safi as she summoned the last remnants of energy to complete her responsibility in the ceremony.

"I pledge my body and mind and will to You, my Master Amenhotep, and happily join as a willing slave in Your House. I am Yours to command, as You wish," safi recited, arousing another applause from the audience.

As I stood in my ceremonial robe to witness this affair, I scanned the room, noticing the Houses that were represented, both locally and nationally, in attendance. I selfishly zeroed in on the area where Neferterri and the girls were, noticing Kitana had also taken her place with them, as commanded. But what also caught my eye as I reluctantly left my area to scan the crowd was unexpected: there was Ice, on his knees, being stroked by Mistress Sinsual while on the opposite side of tiger.

When I made eye contact with Ice to figure out what he was doing with Sin, he lowered his eyes as a submissive would when a Dominant looked in their direction. I *really* needed answers, but first I needed to complete the ceremony, which required one final act on my part.

The act required me to attach the leash to safi's collar, lead her back to the St. Andrews Cross in the dungeon, and publicly invite the other Dominants in attendance to flog her ass and back and on any spot as they wished, as is in keeping with tradition to complete the collaring ceremony.

Before releasing her from my control, I whispered into safi's ear, "Enjoy your experience, little one. you are in good hands with your Master."

"Thank You, m'Lord. i enjoyed my session with You as well, if this one is allowed to say so," she whispered as I placed the blindfold over her eyes. "i am happy i was able to please You also, m'Lord."

I placed a small kiss on her shoulder to provide a silent answer to her appreciation of our time together. I silently walked away as Amenhotep walked over to reclaim His property.

Neferterri was the first to greet me after I left safi. "Okay, did You see Ice over at Sin's area? You know I'm curious how She managed to get him to kneel with tiger during the ceremony."

"No more curious that I am right now, seeing him with Sin at Her feet. But I think we'll have answers in due time. While You go scene with the girls, I will go interrogate our newest submissive about a few things."

We headed back upstairs to the grand room, where Neferterri had left the girls to talk until we returned to them. Upon seeing us approaching them, shamise immediately settled into her kneeling position, with the others following suit.

"Take the girls and head to our room so You can have Your time with them," I told Neferterri as each girl rose to her feet. "Kitana and I need to discuss some things."

Since the pool area had been deserted in favor of the dungeon in the basement, it gave Kitana and me some time to talk alone as friends. I had to switch personas, which meant I was Kane again, just for a few moments because we weren't at a swing party. But it would give her the comfort zone she needed to talk openly.

"Okay, sexy, talk to me. What brought all this on?"

Kitana sat in my lap facing me, straddling my crotch, which aroused me quickly, and while her body begged me to take her, she needed to explain herself and her newfound tendencies.

"Sinsual approached Ice about six months ago, at Your birthday party," she began. "She whispered something in his ear while tiger was servicing one of the Dominas—i think that's the term—in one of the upstairs bedrooms. Next thing i knew, he was on his knees, worshipping Her, letting her do things that he had never let me do to him. At first, it freaked me out because...well, You know Ice."

Yeah, I knew Ice. He was one of the few I sat back and watched because he put on a show. I always wondered if he was trying to be a porn star with the moves he had.

Kitana continued, "Then, for some reason, when i took a closer look at how You were with shamise...the intensity of how You used the flogger on her...the way she called out Your name, and You hadn't even fucked her yet, it got me wet as hell."

"But we had been flirting and I had been teasing you about this for the last year at least." I tried to resist the heat emanating from her body, but I couldn't help it; she was really getting to me. She squirmed in my lap as we talked, and her passion consumed us both. It was only a matter of time before we would have to cut this conversation short.

"Well, remember when Mercedes chose me to be Your birthday present, to be Your slut? When You started to treat me rough, like

You did with nuru…fucking my mouth, pulling my hair, slapping my ass, growling in my ear how good a slut i was for You…i came so hard i had multiple orgasms while You fucked me."

"I really didn't know that. Wow," I uttered. I was speechless.

"Yes, I was so turned on by it all, I started to get high, like I was having an out-of-body experience," she added. "I had to talk to Mercedes to calm down; I was so vulnerable. That's when She told me You had helped me enter subspace."

Once I'd finally gotten some answers, at least for now, I switched back to being Ramesses and told Kitana, "Come, there is something that you need to see."

I took her down to the dungeon, where Amenhotep was busy breaking safi in while her hands and ankles were tied down on a padded work bench, bound in a doggie-style position. He had a leather flogger and was in full motion, slapping along her lower back, her legs, and her ass. Between each slap, one of the slave girls would take a pinwheel and rake it across the area that He worked over with the flogger. safi screamed her head off, begging her Master to give her more.

I took my place behind Kitana as she watched the whole scene unfold. The harder Amenhotep flogged and whipped safi, the louder she became, and the more the other girls encouraged Him to continue. I felt Kitana's heartbeat quicken as I caressed her breasts during the scene, but she didn't moan, as her eyes were fixed on the sights and sounds in front of her.

"Do you like what you see?"

"Yes, i do, my Lord."

"Do you want to feel something like that?"

"Yes, my Lord."

"Is it making you wet, My dear?"

"*Mmmm*...yes, my Lord."

I caressed her ass while Kitana continued to watch. Instinctively, her body leaned into mine, trying not to lose her balance. When I gently tapped her ass, Kitana let out a gasp.

"Harder, please, my Lord. Spank me harder."

SMACK! SMACK! SMACK!

I pulled on her bikini bottom as well, snapping the band against her skin. I slipped the bikini top off her shoulder, exposing her breasts and watching her shiver with delight. I took my fingers and pinched her nipples, making her squirm while in my grasp. I held her in place, torturing her nipples by pinching them harder, waiting for her body to awaken before my eyes.

"Please, more, please," she pleaded. I could barely hear her over the sounds of the scene, closing the space between us before I really got into it.

SMACK! SMACK! SMACK! SMACK! SMACK!

The second series of spankings caused Kitana's legs to weaken, and I knew I had her then. Her hips began gyrating, as if she had been taking exotic dance lessons or something.

Finally, as if in a trance, she turned her head up toward my ear and whispered, "I'm Yours, my Lord. Take me now!"

3 RAMESSES

I'd swear, if I wasn't me, I'd be jealous of me right about now.

Watching Kitana on all fours crawling down the hallway completely naked, except for the heels she wore, was a sight to behold.

Taking notice of all of the other Dominants staring as she swayed her hips and moved as fluidly as a seasoned submissive would made me proud to know she had chosen my Beloved and me as her Dominants. Wary of another Dominant touching her, I stayed closely beside her. Since she did not have a collar, a Dominant could technically still touch her, unless she stayed in close proximity of the Dominant charged with her protection.

She followed me into the bedroom where Neferterri and the girls were performing before a captive audience. Normally, I would have watched them all go at it, but because of what Kitana was doing to Me, I had to release.

"shamise, come to Me, now," I commanded as I pulled her from the outside spot in the ménage she was a part of. She crawled on her hands and knees over to where Kitana and I were standing, quickly moving into her kneeling position.

"Yes, Daddy, what do You command?" she asked on cue.

"you will prepare Me to pleasure Kitana, now," I replied.

"As You wish, Daddy."

As shamise began her task by taking my shaft in hand, I commanded of Kitana, "Help shamise in her task, Kitana."

Kitana never hesitated, entranced the entire time she was with shamise.

The audience that gathered definitely enjoyed the sight that lay before them:

Neferterri had jamii doggie-style on one end of the bed, while nuru took a dildo to jamii from underneath. On the other side, Kitana and shamise took turns sucking me and getting each other wet. Thank God the other master bedroom we normally occupied was big enough to handle the ever expanding crowd, lest someone get a little upset they couldn't see everything going on.

"Do you want to taste her?" I looked in Kitana's eyes while my shaft was still in her mouth.

She nodded, and I motioned for shamise to lie on her back and spread her legs so Kitana could move into position over her exposed wetness.

shamise shook for a couple of seconds after Kitana concentrated on her spot. I grabbed shamise's hair, thrusting my member into her mouth forcefully, knowing it would have her coming in no time. Within a couple of minutes, I felt shamise moaning hard through my thrusts.

"Prepare Kitana for Me, shamise," I ordered.

shamise moved from her position and brought Kitana up on the bed. Whispering in her ear, shamise played with Kitana's breasts, moving down her stomach to playfully slap against her clit. "she's ready for You, Daddy."

Sliding inside of Kitana felt different this time. Her body language was more animated, like her true self had sexually awakened and completely took over. My adrenaline kicked in, matching the intensity of the moment. It wasn't long before the pounding that Kitana took would take effect. shamise noticed as she whispered into Kitana's ear for me to fuck her harder and to beg my permission for her to come.

"Fuck me harder, Sir, please...oh, God, I wanna come, Sir, Please?!?! I feel it coming...

"HARDER!!!" Kitana screamed out, much to the crowd's delight.

I was still in a zone, barely able to do anything more than grunt and nod. But hearing Kitana screaming and shamise in my ear urging me on made me push to pound her even harder.

shamise got up from her spot with Kitana and me to keep an eye on other guests who tried to join into the scene. Having been with us the longest, she knew how to properly express to anyone, Dominant or submissive, that we were not to be disturbed while the session commenced. She approached some of the swinger couples and a couple of single males in the crowd and informed them that their silence was very much appreciated, and they were only allowed to watch until further notice.

Neferterri and nuru finished their interlude, but instead of interrupting, they simply joined jamii and shamise in watching the two of us, as the crowd had been. I wasn't doing anything different, but for some reason, a first sexual experience with a new submissive seems different from first view.

I felt myself building to an orgasm, pulling out immediately and taking off the condom. shamise quickly moved into position and took hold of my girth to jack me off as my orgasm crested, while Kitana sat up to receive my juices on her face and breasts.

"That's it, come on me!" Kitana screamed, taking over from where shamise left off, her eyes wild as my shaft pulsed in her hand. *"i want it all!"*

Kitana then swallowed me whole as I erupted deep inside her mouth and down her throat. She held on to take every drop I gave her until my orgasm finally subsided, which surprised the hell out of me. I didn't know she had those skills. Kitana lay back on the bed, no doubt a little tired from what we had just experienced.

shamise asked, "May i clean Kitana off, Daddy?"

I nodded again, still unable to really speak. jamii slid over from where she was on the bed, and upon seeing I was still dripping from my orgasm, began licking me dry, in hopes of getting me hard again. It felt amazing, especially since I hadn't really gone completely soft, but I needed the down time to gather my thoughts before trying to engage into anything physical for a little while.

I heard a soft applause coming from the crowd before they quietly left the room, leaving us alone to recover. A couple of minutes later, two of Amenhotep's service slave girls entered the room with drinks and towels for us.

Neferterri slid in to straddle her legs behind me to rub my back and shoulders. jamii was still on her knees between my legs, succeeding in her attempt to get me going again, her eyes silently asking for attention from me. Next to us, Kitana and shamise were still kissing and playing with each other, while nuru placed her attention on shamise's clit.

"Will there be anything else that you require of us right now, m'Lord?" I heard one of the service slave girls inquire as they slipped into the room. Having fulfilled their duties for the moment, I could tell they were simply indulging in visual stimulation while their Master wasn't watching.

"No, girls, you will not be needed, I don't think. I will, however, need extra towels for our showers in the morning. I have a feeling we will have one more staying in our room tonight." I looked over at Kitana, who was blushing at that statement, realizing I was speaking about her.

"Yes, as You command, m'Lord. We will return within the hour with the extra towels, as we have to attend to the other guests," the other slave girl stated before they left us in the room.

"So, are you content with the decision that you made, Kitana?" Neferterri asked her.

Kitana was still enjoying shamise's tongue action, and between moans, replied, "Yes, my Lady...God, that's the spot, baby...i want to belong to this House...mmm, damn...i don't want to go anywhere."

☥

I thought I was dreaming...but last night wasn't a dream.

I don't know too many men who would complain about waking up with about five women, including his wife, in bed with him, but that's exactly what I woke up to that morning.

What usually was nearly every straight man's fantasy was my reality.

God, I loved my lifestyle.

I was awakened by a pair of tongues along both sides of my shaft, which was already hard anyway, thanks to the dreams I had earlier that morning. I looked down at the source of my pleasure, and noticed both nuru and jamii were on me at the same time, exchanging kisses in between using their skilled tongues on my shaft.

Since the other girls were still asleep, and I was surprisingly fully recharged after only three hours sleep, we decided to get a good bit of sex in before it was time to go to breakfast. We went at it for a good while before the other girls got up and saw what was going on. I left them to their pleasures amongst themselves as I took jamii into the shower with me so she could cleanse me thoroughly.

The way I felt, I had it in my mind to reward her for making sure her cleaning duties were completed to satisfaction.

As jamii attended to the task at hand, my mind flashed back to Kitana and the previous night's events. To be honest, I had no intentions of acquiring her. I mean, we had our hands full with shamise, jamii, and nuru as it was. But my wife knew how greedy I could be, not to mention my weakness for women with curves. The only thing to do now was to let it ride and enjoy the journey with her.

By then, jamii was nearly finished with her task of washing me completely.

"Thank you, My pet, you have performed your task thoroughly. Do you want your pleasure now or later on today, jamii?" I asked her, bringing her to her feet.

"May i request later, Sir? To be honest, i am kind of sore from everything Goddess did to me last night," jamii replied sheepishly.

"Yes, you may request for later, little one." I wasn't disappointed. I kind of needed a break as well, especially after she and nuru wore me out not twenty minutes earlier.

As we were getting dressed, Kitana came to me, eyes lowered, and said, "That was one of the most intense nights that i have had in a long time, Sir. Did i please You last night?"

I kissed her forehead, looked into her hazel eyes and whispered, "I think you felt your answer in your mouth last night, little one."

Kitana blushed, smiling brightly at the thought of what she'd experienced.

"i'd better get back to my husband before brunch so we can talk. Hopefully Mistress has released him this morning," she stated, quietly slipping out of the room.

"I think Kitana's still tingling from what You did to her last night."

My wife's grin and pleasant demeanor let me know that she'd enjoyed herself watching me.

"Yes, my Lord, it brought back memories of our first times with You," nuru mentioned.

"shamise and i were talking about that before we went to sleep."

shamise added, "i really like this one, Daddy. It's like she fit right in with us last night. Is she going to be a part of our House?"

"I believe so, baby. she asked to be included last night, but I want to make sure after breakfast if she understands what that means," I told her. While I was curious about what was really happening at that point, if I'd learned anything, it's that this lifestyle brought a lot of surprises. All you could do was be prepared for every one of them.

Unfortunately, that mantra would be put to the test once we stepped out of our bedroom to join the remaining attendees for brunch.

4 RAMESSES

Tension was never a good thing to have late in the morning.

The atmosphere in the grand dining room greeted us with the force and unrelenting chill of a snowstorm. I was hoping it was all a figment of my imagination, but I relied on my ability to sense the vibe and energy amongst a group of people. The way I felt at that exact moment, we should have packed up the cars and made a break for the house.

Almost as soon as we entered, the tension in the air gave me pause. I tried hard to grasp the source of the tension, as none of the slave girls were willing to acknowledge it as they went about their morning routines. I searched the room for any traces of the bliss I'd enjoyed the previous night, but there was none to be found. I finally spotted tiger, a very disturbing expression on his face. His body language tripped Neferterri's senses. Mistress Sinsual was somewhere irritated, to say the least.

"I'm going to find Sin. This can't be good." Neferterri walked out of the room hastily. Not that I blamed her. I wanted to have something better to do, too.

After the girls got settled into their seats, I looked over at Amenhotep, who was His usual casual self. He had to feel the vibe released into the room. I looked at a few of the other Dominas who'd stayed overnight with their submissives, and from their body language, I could tell that they were doing their best to ignore and get through it. I couldn't quite place what was going on, but I had a feeling that someone had really messed up.

As the other slave girls began serving breakfast, I continued my search, finally locating Ice and Kitana engaged in a very intense conversation. Kitana was visibly irate about something, and judging from the look on her face, something didn't feel right. She would be coming by the house later on, so I figured we would get the details then.

Neferterri and Mistress Sinsual finally re-entered the room. Sin shot a very frosty look at Ice before she took her place with tiger at the table. Neferterri didn't look happy either upon returning to the girls and me. Rather than push the issue, I concluded one very easy point: Ice really had fucked up, and he was really going to be severely punished for it. Sin's sadistic side was nothing to fool around with. That probably explained why the tension was so thick. Sin rarely ever showed public displeasure, period. It wasn't her style.

Amenhotep stood up with safi and paka at His sides, and He raised the glass of Mimosa in His hand to propose a few words.

Everyone looked in my direction, thinking maybe Amenhotep was pointing His glass at me to say a few words of my own before He began. Instead, I rose to my feet, pointing my glass toward Him, to join Him in whatever He was about to say. The rest of the crowd followed my lead, grabbing their glasses as well, waiting for Amenhotep to speak.

"I want to thank you all for bearing witness to the collaring of the newest addition to My House, safi. I believe she will be as valuable as all My girls are, especially My paka." Amenhotep looked at paka with an appreciation rarely seen publicly. I also saw something else in His eyes as He looked at paka, something I really needed to be clear about before asking Him, but now was not the time.

"I would hope you are all available for the Halloween party in a little over a month or so. It will be a masquerade party, of course, and the naughtier the better. Please be safe on your way home."

My cell phone went off as soon as the speech was over. When I checked the text message, it was enough to make me grit my teeth in irritation.

"Okay, what happened now?" Neferterri asked.

I showed her the text, which was from Jay:

Jasmine's flipped out again, dawg. Need a spot to crash. I will explain later.

"What did he do now?" she asked. I think she wondered if Jay was asking for it half the time.

"I don't know, baby, but I'm sure he's got an excuse for this one, too."

☥

God it was good to be home.

After picking up the kids and finally getting through the door, Neferterri and I had really planned on relaxing and maybe watch a little football. We weren't expecting Kitana for a few hours since she and her husband were at the Falcons game. But unfortunately that wasn't to be the case because Jay rang the doorbell before we could get settled in.

"He's not staying here this time, baby." She was adamant about the issue and for the first time in a while, I was in agreement with her.

Lately, it was the same thing every few months:

Have a party.

Jasmine gets drunk.

Jay does his thing during the party, which pisses Jasmine off because she's not having fun.

Jay gets put out of the house for her insecurities, regardless of what he does.

Jay needs a place to crash for the night, and the last couple of times, it's been our house.

Well, the lady of the house had spoken, and the four words for the day were: *listen to your woman.*

"Okay, Jay, what happened this time?"

"Mercedes, it's not what you think," Jay protested. "She's bugging out, accusing me of cheating on her and shit. I don't know what she's on, but you know me."

Neferterri softened her stance a little bit. Jay could be a lot of things, but a cheating husband was not one of them, and even she knew it. He loved the hell out of Jasmine, but it's a little deeper now, and I think it had everything to do with the little sexy secretary who worked in his division at his job.

I didn't want her to jump to conclusions if I mentioned the secretary right then, so I went in a different direction. "Maybe you both need to take a break from the scene for a while, until things calm down between you."

I hoped to get him to understand where I was going with that last statement. I mean, sometimes the lifestyle can cause more problems than it can solve, especially if the foundation of the relationship wasn't strong to begin with. Hell, we've stepped away a couple of times to take an extended break, the last time being the birth of our youngest daughter four years ago.

"You might be right, dawg, but it's hard to get away sometimes, especially when a brotha is missed." Jay let his ego come into play, and I felt for him. This lifestyle can be addictive, and we're all addicted at one point in time, but in life, you have decisions that have to be made. I just hoped he had enough sense to make enough good ones. Life could be long if you didn't.

"Look, Jay, please go home and talk to her. Jasmine loves you, but you have things that need to be worked out." Neferterri dropped a big hint on Jay, letting him know there was no vacancy this time around.

Surprisingly, he took the hint. "Yeah, maybe she'll listen this time," Jay replied. "Look, I'm sorry if I ruined your evening, but there is only so much a brotha can take."

5 & RAMESSES

Kitana was at the house a couple of hours later.

She looked even more beautiful than she did last night, her Falcons jersey and blue jeans hugging her in all the right places. She stood like she wasn't sure how to approach me. She chewed on her bottom lip again, which I increasingly found sexier each time I saw it.

"Good afternoon, Ka…Sir…okay, now I'm confused as to how to address you now."

Kitana came through the door with a bit of her own confusion showing on her pretty face. "I know I have a lot to learn, but I'm serious about this."

After everything that had transpired at the Palace this weekend, it really gave me a new sense of confusion and excitement all at the same time. On the one hand, I couldn't have asked for a better acquisition. Kitana was a blank canvas for the most part, a lifestyle Dominant's dream, especially one as jaded as I felt I had become. She would absorb every lesson that Neferterri and I would teach her, and there was no residual "baggage" from a previous Dominant to re-program a submissive from.

On the other hand, I was concerned I was stretching myself too thin, and that was the other side of the equation. We already had three submissives; to add a fourth would really be a bit greedy on my part, but at the moment I really didn't care. Our girls were devoted to us, and they understood before they submitted, this was a Poly family endeavor, not a one-on-one situation. I've never made any apologies for being who I was, and I'd be damned if I was going to start now.

"First, Kitana, we're not in a D/s environment, so no need to think you're supposed to act accordingly," I answered, giving her a warm hug. "Second, I'm still the same friend you have always known. You're just getting the rare opportunity to see another side of both me and Mercedes now."

"Thanks, Kane, I really needed that." Kitana melted into the hug a little more than I was prepared for. Something was up.

I won't lie, she felt good to the touch…really good.

"Okay, Kitana, what's going on with you? I mean, usually just seeing me lights up your face." I tried to be light to keep her spirits up, especially after dealing with Jay's crazy ass.

"That's why I love you, Kane, I wouldn't let anyone else dictate my moods the way you do," she replied, her eyes starting to sparkle a little bit as she looked up at me. "To answer your question, last night was one of the most…intense…*damn*…erotic nights I've ever had in my life. I think that's what's bothering me so much. It shook me to my core…scared the hell out of me. But now, I feel so… blah."

I guess I expected this to hit a little later in the week, and I was prepared for it to happen then, not now.

Sub drop. She showed the signs, even without communicating them to me.

The euphoria of the weekend really got her so high that she was literally floating, dare I say she was flying. Then, to have to deal with the realities of what she had experienced, and after witnessing the drama that ensued between her and Ice, I guess I should have known the crash was going to be rather destructive.

Here I was thinking this would be a normal Sunday afterglow. Oh well, such is the life of a Poly Dominant.

Neferterri walked into the living room, and she picked up on Kitana's vibe. One look at her and she exhaled, blowing her bangs in the air. "God, we were hoping you wouldn't crash until mid-week. For that matter, what happened between you and Ice? I imagine that's got you crashing sooner than we expected you to."

"Mercedes, he lost it this morning," Kitana began. "I mean, trying to get details about what we did, and then he got pissed because I couldn't give details of what happened last night. shamise explained that IT was one of the House rules, so I made sure to stick to the rules, even if it meant not telling Ice. Hell, he knows, because Sinsual goes by the same rules."

Kitana was right. To keep down on copycat nonsense, most Dominants usually kept their submissives under a gag order, except for pictures, while others who like to showcase their skills will allow their submissives to be live "mouthpieces" for the community to take notice. But for this House, all of the girls know not to speak of the goings-on once it had been deemed private play.

"Do you need me to speak to Sin for you, baby? I have a feeling Ice thought he could tell you what he did and it would guilt you into telling what you did. But he has to realize this isn't swinging. There are rules and protocol to follow, and he has to be made to understand that," Neferterri told her. "Hell, he shouldn't have said a word to you about what happened with Sin. That was a breach of Her protocol."

"I understand, but I think Ice thought this was another kinky thing to get off on. I don't even think he's even serious about submitting to Sin the way I'm serious about submitting to the two of you," Kitana answered. "I'm still floating for the most part, but he almost ruined my buzz."

I laughed, but my buzz walked right out the door to put it mildly. I was halfway expecting one of the other girls to either call or instant message to let either me or Mercedes know they were coming down and in need of comfort as well.

I grabbed one of the blankets from the hall closet to put over Neferterri and Kitana to keep her warm. One of the things a Dominant had to protect against when a submissive goes through sub drop is when they experienced chills. While her skin was warm to the touch, I felt Kitana trembling, and so did Neferterri.

"Thank you both for being here. I really didn't know how to deal with what was happening to me," Kitana said, leaning her head against Neferterri's shoulder. "I thought I was going nuts for a minute."

"You will be fine, baby, it will pass, I promise." Neferterri comforted her to keep her from crashing harder. She held Kitana for a good thirty minutes while I kept up with the girls and explained to them that "Auntie Kitana" got a little sick and mommy was taking care of her for a little while. Considering the girls were used to both of us being affectionate and hyper around our friends, they didn't see as anything more than "much ado about nothing."I didn't want to see this as a precursor of things to possibly come in the future, but sometimes there's not much choice in the matter. I knew one thing: I was going to enjoy some football today or someone was going to pay with their lives.

☥

Monday morning came and was going pretty well and it was also my day off.

I went through the usual routine once the wife and kids were out of the house: check email, do the marketing for the next event night, and go through the other pages of the girls to see who was trying to connect. This Monday would be a little different, because I needed to set up Kitana's page and screen name. It's a small price to pay for having to work most Saturdays, but having a weekday off had its advantages.

While online, I found out through several offline messages of our girls' screen names that some men wanted to get with them, and as quickly as they asked, they received the automatic reply that they would have to go through me or Neferterri for permission. Since neither one of us had really received any offline messages over the weekend, I guess none of the men were "man" enough to ask for what they wanted from a collared submissive. Oh well, not my fault. As far as I was concerned, closed mouths don't get fed.

Still, some have given us a bit of grief for having that particular rule in place. While there might seem like there's insecurity rooted within, nothing could be further from the truth. We're very protective of our girls, and we make no apologies for making sure the risk of diseases was mitigated as much as we could manage. Think about it: would you want someone else haphazardly playing with your toys and then returning them in any old condition?

Yeah, I didn't think so, either.

I finally got back to our profile and screen name on messenger, sending thank you notes for attending safi's collaring on behalf of Amenhotep. He didn't really get into all the online stuff, saying that it's too much for Him to deal with. But he was an old school Dominant, the so-called "Old Guard" Leather, before advent of the Internet, when word of mouth was the only way to get noticed. He swears all this "internet stuff" was too advanced for Him, but I knew better. In some respects, I'm still His apprentice, and I ended up doing some of the grunt work that He didn't want to do.

I was in the middle of setting up Kitana's page on FetLife, when a message window popped up. Upon further inspection, I noticed it was another Dom contacting me.

master_gee: *Good morning to You, Sir.*

lord_ramesses: *Good morning to You as well, Sir.*

master_gee: *I am a new Dom to the city, Sir. Mistress Blaze told Me that You were the person to contact*

lord_ramesses: *I thank Mistress for referring You to Me, Master Gee. What information do you seek?*

master_gee: *I am curious as to whether or not You have any submissives that may be of service to Me, Sir?*

My first instinct was he must be new. Any experienced Dominant would already have the information on a submissive they were interested in; he would only need to come to me to see if I would vet for the submissive in question or not. The way this one sounded, he wanted me to hand one over on a silver platter. I decided to play this out, to see where this went.

lord_ramesses: *Where did You move from, Master Gee?*

master_gee: *I am from Texas, trained and converted by Master Q-Sun. I'm certain that You know of Him, Sir.*

lord_ramesses: *Yes, I am. He and I trained under the same Domina. Is He aware that You are in Atlanta?*

I should have known this "Master Gee" was new. Q-Sun had a

weakness for training a protégé. I was almost about to read him the riot act, but I guess he saw it coming.

master_gee: *Begging Your forgiveness, Lord Ramesses. Master told Me that You would realize that I was following His instructions and that You would know that He was behind this.*

I laughed at the screen, barely containing the noise I made. This was vintage Q. I made a mental note to call him later on in the week. He usually let me know when one of his relocates, and vice-versa.

I kept the conversation going to see what Q had taught him when the phone rang. Looking at the caller ID, I shook my head. *Why in the hell is she calling me?*

My afternoon was about to get very frustrating.

"I'm sorry to disturb you, Kane, but have you seen Jay?" Jasmine asked the one question I really didn't want to answer.

"Jasmine, I haven't seen or talked to him since last night, after you booted him out of the house *again*."

Like my boy said, *there's only so much a bruh can take.*

"Kane, spare me the drama. Where's my husband?" She tried to sound angry, but there was an irritated tone in her voice. It wasn't anger I sensed in her tone. It was fear. But what was she scared of?

"Jasmine, he's not at my house, and quite frankly, I wouldn't answer your calls either," I snapped back.

"I should have known he couldn't keep his damn mouth shut." Jasmine hung up the phone before I could grasp what she'd just said. "Never mind, I'll find him myself."

I couldn't figure out what the hell that was about, but if she couldn't find him in the usual spots, maybe Jay had had enough of the bad treatment after all. Knowing Jay, he was screening his calls at work, and if Jasmine was calling me looking for him, then maybe he really didn't want her finding him. Quite frankly, I was worried, because Jay might have reached the end of his rope. There was no telling what, or who, for that matter, he could have been doing at that point.

I was not in the mood for having my mind twisted over nonsense, so I dismissed the call and went back to my online "to-do list." The phone rang again, and I was shocked to see Candy's name and home phone number come across the screen, especially the time of the day when I knew she's supposed to be at work.

"What are you doing home, baby? Are you feeling okay?" I asked out of concern.

"No, I'm not feeling well, Daddy." There was a playful tone in her voice; I heard it clearly. She was in a sensual mood. "I'm hot, feverish. I think I need something to break this fever, Daddy."

I couldn't resist a role play with Candy, no more than I could with Mercedes. There was a reason why she's my "concubine," although it's a harsh term for most folks to understand. She's much more than that to the both of us.

"I'm trying to relax, baby, I really didn't plan on coming out of the house today. You know I had a rough weekend with the party and all." I played along with the flow to see where things would go.

"I know, Daddy, but I didn't get to feel you this weekend. You know I can only go so long without feeling you deep inside of me," she cooed. "I'm naked on my bed, and just hearing your voice has me wet."

My mind immediately envisioned Candy splayed spread-eagle on her bed, showing off her flexibility, fingers slowly spreading her lips apart to allow her aroma to fill the room.

"I've got my fingers rubbing my clit for you, Daddy." She kept up her onslaught, purring into my ear and releasing a few moans for effect.

All of a sudden, the list I was planning to complete didn't seem so pressing.

Hearing Candy's coos and moans had my senses in a frenzied state. I could already feel my nature growing, and I thanked heaven I'd worn sweat pants. I wanted to lose myself in the storm she was creating, but there was no way I was going to let her control the flow. Call me a control freak if you want, but quite frankly, I didn't really give a fuck.

"Did I tell you that you could touch yourself?" I forcefully asked, hearing a pause over the phone as I took control.

"No, Daddy," I heard Candy whisper over the phone. "But I missed you so much. You haven't tapped this ass in a month, and I was beginning to think you didn't want me anymore."

I loved the way she begged, loved the way she pouted. It was my one weakness as a man, to be needed for your strength, virility. I hated I still had some weaknesses that could be exploited, but at the same time, took relief I still felt human. Sometimes as a Dominant, I tended to feel like I had ice water in my veins, like I didn't need to feel any vulnerability.

"I see now I need to remind you of who owns that pretty ass of yours, don't I?" I dropped my voice a couple of octaves for effect, felt Candy shiver over the phone.

"Yes, Daddy, you know I keep it good and tight for you." She always knew the words to keep my mind running and keep me revved up. "I'm spoiled, and it's all your fault."

I chuckled at her remark. Some things I can't help, seeing as they come naturally to me. There's nothing like being a Southern Gentleman…*nothing.*

"*Te quiero, papi,*" Now she wanted to break out the Spanish. Damn. "*Quiero sentirte dentro de mi.*"

Basically and bluntly speaking, without translating too much, my bitch was in heat, and her heat needed to be extinguished something terrible.

"*Papi te ama tambien, niña*," I said in return, but considering I wasn't leaving the house, I had to calm her down and make her understand that there would be time for us soon. Such is the way of things, and she knows I make it worth the wait. "I want you off work on Wednesday so I can make sure you won't have to beg for at least the next couple of weeks; do you understand me?"

Candy kept moaning on the phone as she responded to my request. "Yes, Daddy. Do I have permission to keep it wet and tight for you until Wednesday?"

"Yes, and make sure you either find or shop for the proper outfit to greet me in as well. I know you won't disappoint; you never do," I told her before getting off the phone. No matter how badly we both needed the release, I needed the rest more. I didn't like cheating any of our girls, and I was not about to start now. Besides, it was part of what makes me, well, me.

I plopped down on the couch to catch up on some fictional drama for a while. The wife and kids would be home soon, and I needed to prepare for the onslaught in the form of our daughters. Sometimes it was a little more fun to watch other people do dirt, I had to admit. It was one of the few guilty pleasures I had in life, and I was loathed to give them up.

My thoughts turned to Jay the moment I turned the television on to watch *The Game* on BET. I hadn't heard anything from him, despite the perception of my little white lie to his wife. I needed to get in touch with him, figure out why he hadn't gotten back with anyone.

Neferterri walked through the door with the kids in tow as I left a message for Jay to get back to me ASAP.

"Hey, baby, how was your day?" she asked as our youngest daughter jumped into my arms.

"Do you want the fun or drama?" I asked her back.

"Fun first, I'm in a good mood," Mercedes answered.

"One of Q's newly trained moved here and got in touch with me."

Mercedes rolled her eyes. "I hope this one is at least house-broken. Now, what drama has happened?"

"Jay's M.I.A., it might be for real this time. Jasmine even called me looking for him." I stated.

This smirk spread across her face as she shifted her weight onto her back foot. "You mean I might know something the great Lord Ramesses doesn't?" She even put a hand on her hip to really lay it on thick.

Usually I didn't switch personas in front of the kids, but she really left me no choice. I popped her across her ass with force and asked, "You might know what, exactly?"

Mercedes shuddered briefly, answering quickly, "He's at the Airport Marriott with Mistress Blaze's slut, Beloved."

That meant Jay was being drained dry by jezzabelle, Mistress Blaze's insatiable slut. Blaze only lets her out in emergency situations because of her sexual appetite, and she doesn't do it for strangers, which meant Jay used my name to get her to do it. In fact, I knew for fact she still had jezzabelle in chaste for at least another week.

"Well, damn, this must have been one helluva situation to let Her out early." I grabbed my keys. "I'll be back in an hour."

6 RAMESSES

I really didn't want to imagine the worst, but sometimes a man reaches the point of no return, and my boy certainly was no different.

Jay opened the door to the hotel suite wearing boxers and a robe, looking high as a kite from the weed he had been smoking. That tipped me off that something was really off. Jay doesn't smoke weed, mainly because his company does random drug tests at least once a month.

"You want some of this, K? She's been off the chain since she got here. I need a break."

My attention turned to jezzabelle, in a bowing position, and spread out doggie-style on the bed. She swayed her hips in anticipation of servicing another person.

Needless to say, I was highly pissed. To be so damned reckless…

Without answering him, I walked over to where she was and pulled her out of her trance. "Get dressed, little one, and tell your Mistress Lord Ramesses says thank you for allowing you out for this emergency," I commanded. "I will request She keeps you out of your belt for a few more days as reward."

"Yes, my Lord, i will do as You command." she replied before getting into the shower to clean up.

"Damn, is it like that, K? She just got started." Jay sounded upset.

The next thing he felt was my fist against his ribs. I knew he didn't expect it because he dropped to one knee. Thank God he was blazed, or I probably wouldn't have been able to catch him slipping.

"What the fuck was that for?"

"That was for cheating on your wife," I replied, shaking my hand in slight pain. "What the fuck were you thinking?"

"I was thinking about getting pussy the way I *wanted* it," he finally stood up, still holding his ribs. "That bitch was exactly what the doctor ordered."

jezzabelle, who was still in her submissive mental state, heard the last comment Jay made. Thank goodness she still was, or it could have gotten ugly. The last thing a woman wanted was to be called out of her name. A submissive doesn't care while they're in a "slut" mindset. If anything, while in that mindset, they actually get turned on by it.

To keep her intact so she didn't have any residual memory, I immediately stepped in front of her to ensure her submissive side was still there.

"What you heard was a figment of your imagination. Do you understand Me, little one?"

Her eyes lowered, confirming her response.

I kissed her forehead and commanded, "Go and see your Mistress now, and inform Her of My request. you may leave now."

That put her in a better mood before I let her leave the room. I turned my attention back to Jay, who seemed amused by what had happened.

"Man, you and Fillmore Slim need to teach classes on this shit." Jay smirked. That got him another jab to the gut.

"You know, even with the way Jasmine acts sometimes, you can really be a jackass," I scolded. "Besides, I'm not a pimp."

"Whatever, K, what did you come here for anyway?" It wasn't until then I realized he had been drinking on top of smoking weed. The smell from Mary Jane hid the liquor on his breath.

"Okay, man, lay it down for me. What's going on? This ain't like you to fall off the wagon or some shit like this?"

"Man, you know what? Listening to your woman was probably the best thing I could have done. Otherwise, I would have never caught her ass fucking two dudes in my house last night."

That bomb took my breath away. Sure, been there, done that, but a woman doing it for no reason? That explained Jasmine's voice earlier. She'd been caught stealing third base. Actually, she'd been caught stealing third base while another one slid into home.

"What the fuck?"

"You know the wild part? She made it sound like it was my fault, dawg. Can you believe that shit? She's the one butt ass naked, in the middle of a threesome, and I'm the one who gets blamed. So, I called Blaze up, explained the situation to Her, told Her I needed to release, and ol' girl was at my door within the hour."

Things were not adding up. I wanted to believe for him he was just seeing things. For the first time in a long time, I was speechless.

Jay continued his rant. "I busted my ass this whole time, just so she could fuck me over. I should've killed her!"

"Slow down, J, you kept your cool, be thankful for that. We could have been having this same convo with you behind bars." I had to remind him.

Damn. How did it come to this?

"K, you're my boy and I love you like a brother. I'm a lot of things, but I'm not a killer."

Feeling he was cooling off, I asked him, "So, what's your next move?"

The answer came in the form of a knock on the door. When he opened it, two more women were standing there looking like they were pleased to see him standing there. I recognized them immediately, remembering them from a couple of months ago. They usually partied with us whenever we were at Candy's house hosting.

Jay had to get this hurt out of his system before anything could go further, and I knew it. Hell, I'd probably be doing the same thing right now. One thing was for certain: it was going to get worse before it got better. But I wasn't so sure it would get better this time.

☥

"I'm here, as you asked, Daddy."

Seeing Candy at my door in next to nothing except a pair of heels was definitely what the doctor ordered. I needed to get my mind off of the bullshit yesterday with Jay, but I had a feeling she needed some help, too, so I made Neferterri call in to work this morning. I wasn't feeling well and needed to go to the doctor.

Yeah, weak excuse, I know. But I was in need of some sexual healing.

"Come to me," I commanded.

"Yes, Daddy," she replied, closing the door behind her and repositioning herself on her knees at my feet.

"Were you a good girl while Daddy was away?" I asked her.

"Yes, Daddy," Candy replied. "I kept it wet and tight for you, as you specified."

I looked down at Candy as she untied and removed my shoes and then moved up my pants to unbuckle my belt. "I have a surprise for you, baby," I told her. I lifted her chin up to look at me.

She nodded, never slowing down in her task. She didn't notice Neferterri above her, removing my shirt. My guess was I wouldn't stop them from eventually wanting to get the morning started earlier than I wanted to. Once she noticed her best friend was there with us, the smile on her face was precious, to say the least.

The morning just turned up, to take a phrase from our oldest daughter.

"Hi, baby. Miss me, too?" Neferterri asked her.

"Mmm-hmmm," Candy mouthed, successful in her task of getting my pants off and taking up the new task of her latest oral presentation to the chairman of the board.

My body betrayed me. It had been a couple of days since I'd had sex with Neferterri, and while I promised Candy she would belong to me today, my plans were about to be altered a little bit.

They both had me completely naked in no time, as Candy began to nuzzle her lips against my shaft. Neferterri did not disappoint, either, gently biting and sucking on my nipples, all while coaxing Candy to begin performing her expert deep throat skills on me.

Damn. Candy had me coming in her mouth before I knew what hit me, and she made sure she swallowed every drop I had to give her. I let out a loud primal growl as I erupted, a sound Neferterri was all too familiar with.

I forced Neferterri to her knees and commanded Candy by uttering the single command, "spread." Candy quickly lay on her back and spread her legs on the mattress.

Now, I know what you may be thinking... Neferterri's a Dominant, right?

Why, yes, yes, she is, and a damn good one, too.

Let me clear it up for you: Candy was in the know, but she's not a lifestyle submissive; she simply likes the role play with us, and my wife does like to switch to submissive from time to time as well. So, consider today one of those times, and enjoy the rare view into something like this because it's not likely to happen anytime soon.

I next issued the command to Neferterri, "69," and she straddled her legs and positioned her pussy lips over Candy's face, sitting on her tongue before she dropped down over Candy's silken wetness to complete the command.

While they were busy bringing each other to exquisite pleasure, it allowed me time to compose myself and focus on what I had originally planned to do. I made sure the wax was in its place, still heating on the bar counter top in the kitchen, before I went downstairs and looked around the basement, checking one wall that housed the glass cases of weaponry I used for knife play: knives, swords, smaller switchblades and the like. On the opposite wall were the Saint Andrews Cross and the floggers, bullwhips, and electro-stimulation equipment.

I moved to the wall of floggers and picked out my leather floggers to use on them while they were engaged in each other. The screams I heard from upstairs hurried my steps before they wore themselves out. I still had plans for both of them.

I slapped the flogger against my wife's beautiful ass first, since she was the one on top, increasing the intensity with each stroke across her skin. I heard her moaning while she lapped away at Candy's sex, which only inspired me to flog her harder to elicit a more audible response. I alternated the slaps of the flogger with gentle rakes across her skin with my nails, concentrating on the same area I'd just struck, knowing it would give Mercedes the tingling sensation that would have her coming in no time.

Her ass swayed in rhythmic sync with my flogging and Candy's oral skills; it wouldn't take long to stroke her into an intense orgasm. I quickly mounted her while Candy licked her, and within a few minutes, the stimulation overload pushed her over the edge into her first orgasmic wave.

"*Oh my God, I'm coming, I'm coming!*" my wife yelled out. "*Fuck me harder, Daddy!*"

I kept stroking her, feeling Candy's fingers massaging my balls while I pumped away at Neferterri's swollen lips. Every so often, I pulled out of my wife and slid my dick into Candy's mouth, allowing her to taste us both before penetrating Neferterri again. I finally pulled out a final time so Candy could work Neferterri's clit and make her come again.

Surprisingly, I was still hard. Not as hard as I was when we first got started, but hard enough to get one final climax.

I whispered the command, "sit," into Neferterri's ear, which meant for her to face sit over Candy, leaving Candy's pussy and ass exposed. I walked into the kitchen and took the wax from the counter top, returning to the living room before my wife got any ideas to change positions, and began to drip small slivers of wax onto her exposed clit.

I heard small muffled moans coming from Candy, but she did not lose her concentration. I asked my wife, "Does she want more? Her body says yes, but I want her to say it."

Neferterri tried to form the words, but Candy had her on the edge again. "Yes…fuck…Daddy…she wants more. She's…mmm, dammit…nodding her head. Give her more, Daddy."

I increased the amount of wax, but kept the same cadence, covering her thighs and panty line. Candy gyrated and wiggled her hips, enjoying every minute of the torture I gave her. I used a warm, damp cloth to wipe away the wax that had hardened, but after a while of seeing her pussy begging to be fucked, my body finally heeded the call to duty.

Candy was so wet from the wax torture it was as easy to enter her as it was Neferterri. I didn't stay in her wetness too long, however, because I had something special in mind to bring her to climax.

I commanded Neferterri to crawl and retrieve the dildo she used with her strap-on harness and to get it lubed up.

"Beg me to fuck your ass, Candy," I ordered her. "Tell me how bad you want it in your ass, bitch."

"Please, Daddy, fuck my ass!" Candy screamed. *"It's yours, Daddy, it's all yours!"*

While Mercedes lubed the dildo, I slid a pillow under Candy's ass and slowly penetrated her anally, grinning as I managed to get my entire length inside her. She loved anal sex with either of us. It didn't matter to her who had her, as long as she could fly over the edge and into the abyss of orgasmic bliss. I stroked her slow, allowing her to adjust to my girth, when she received the surprise I had waiting on her.

Mercedes teased Candy's lips with the head of the dildo before inserting it deep into her depths. Candy's eyes widened to the unexpected double penetration euphoria we don't do very often because it triggers powerful multiple orgasms.

I adjusted Candy's hips so we could stroke her without getting in each other's way. With one hand, Mercedes feverishly stroked her pussy, and with the other hand, she pinched Candy's nipples hard, causing her to scream out for her to pinch them harder. I kept stroking her ass, so slick from the friction and lube, it felt like I was inside her wetness.

"You're making me come! Oh my God, yes, I'm coming!" Candy

shrieked, grabbing Neferterri's arm to brace against the intensity of the waves rippling through her body.

I pumped harder, fueled by screams, trying to stave off my own climax building with each stroke. I pulled out before Candy passed out and took the condom off so I could come in my wife's mouth. The feeling was delicious, as her tongue massaged my shaft to prolong the orgasm a little while longer before I pulled out of her mouth.

We collapsed on the floor, completely spent. We were all going to need a nap before we had to go get the kids from school.

"So, what was that about needing a fire put out, baby girl?" Neferterri joked to Candy.

"I'm not complaining anymore," was her response. "You two are more than enough for me for a few days at least."

7 NEFERTERRI

I hated days like this, where I had to walk on eggshells.

Seeing my husband in a funk for the rest of the week, despite the wonderful time we'd had with Candy yesterday, was not something I was used to, and I wasn't about to get used to it, either. This thing with Jay had him disturbed, but he had his moments where he blocked everything and everyone out until he figured out how to fix it. This wasn't going to be an easy fix because of the people involved.

Yeah, I know, being in the lifestyle blurs the lines of monogamy and fidelity, but being dishonest to the one you love and are committed was wrong, period. It's why relationships had to be strong before entering this realm. We'd seen couples who thought they were committed to each other, only to realize they were not sexually compatible to each other. Say what you want, but sex is as important in a relationship as any other aspect, otherwise, the divorce rate wouldn't be so high these days.

He hadn't been neglecting me or the kids or anything. He had the ability to turn off whatever was bothering him for short periods of time. I gave him space when he needed it, especially when Jay came over to shoot pool in the basement. Sometimes it took a man to help another man through his struggles, and I always loved Ramesses for being able to be there for Jay.

Jay had now been gone from Jasmine for nearly two weeks. Even though he was the one wronged in this latest incident, he still tried to swallow his pride and patch things up with her, but he still stayed with different friends the entire time. While it was nice to have him over and he was always great company, sooner or later, something had to give before my home eventually became a battleground for something akin to the "War of the Roses."

Remember how that turned out? Yeah, those were my sentiments exactly.

Ramesses was in the kitchen cooking on a rare Sunday night, doing his own spaghetti concoction the kids seemed to like a lot. The way he joked with the kids and moved around the kitchen, it felt like the whole situation was behind him. I had to be sure, so, at the risk of upsetting the positive vibe in the house, I began my Q&A session.

"Can I ask a question?" I asked him, wrapping my arms around his waist as he sprinkled the chopped onions over the ground beef.

"As long as it has nothing to do with Jasmine, fire away," he answered flatly.

"Baby, I know what she did was fucked up, but she's paying for it."

He put the spatula down, which I already knew was not a good sign. I felt his shoulders tense up, and it was only a matter of bracing for impact from that point forward.

Before he could get a word out, the phone rang. I didn't care who it was, I was happy to not have to hear him roar yet. I left him in the kitchen and grabbed one of the other extensions before one of the kids picked it up.

"Hello?"

"Mercedes, it's Candy. Jasmine's on her way over here." I heard the irritation in her voice. Candy and Jasmine were sorors, but they weren't exactly as tight as they once were. I knew my best friend, and she didn't like being bothered on Sundays. That was, unless it's me or Ramesses.

"I'm on my way." I figured I could deal with my husband's mood once I got done ripping Jasmine a new hole. Imagine my surprise to see my husband and kids laughing at something on TV when I walked into the living room. He acted like the previous ten minutes never happened.

"Baby, I need to head out. I'll be at Candy's, okay?" I shouted out in his direction.

"Yeah, babe, let me know how it turns out," he replied. He was still huddled up with the kids, watching some craziness on television they'd roped him in to watching.

Now, why in the back of my mind did I think he had been listening in on the other extension to make a comment like that?

☥

Thankfully, I got to Candy's house before Jasmine did.

I hoped to beat her there so it didn't look as if she had called me over. To make it less suspicious, I parked my car in the empty garage spot, to make it look like I had been there for a few hours.

The things I do for that woman.

I found Candy sunbathing naked out on the back patio. I stared at her skin as it bronzed in the sun, watching the beads of sweat make her look absolutely radiant enough to rape on the spot. I had to regain my composure though. If I didn't, things might end up rolling into a different flow, and Jasmine's doorbell rings might get ignored. But I shook it off, considering her balcony was in direct line of sight for more than a few neighbors to get a good show. Not like I cared, but sooner or later, she's gonna get busted for indecent exposure.

"So, what did you really need me for?" I asked, knowing she could handle Jasmine on her own.

"Well, I was hoping we could play around and little before she showed up. You know I handle things better when I have some of you." Candy flirted. She moved toward me, ready to get a quickie in. "It has been a couple of weeks, sexy."

The doorbell interrupted that idea quickly.

"Damn," Candy shouted. "You're not getting off that easy. Let's get this over with, but you're gonna have to come out of those clothes if you're gonna fool Jasmine."

I didn't need to be convinced, especially when I was used to being naked at her house. I gave her a quick pop on her ass and said, "Now, go and answer the door."

Once we headed back inside, I managed to slip into the bedroom to put a robe on while Candy let Jasmine in. She cleaned up pretty well, but then again, she probably went to church this afternoon, too. Her demeanor seemed a bit softer than I expected. Considering she hadn't seen her husband for more than a couple of hours for the last couple of weeks, one would think she would at least be on edge.

Candy started up right away, asking, "You still haven't seen Jay?"

"I'd imagine Mercedes has seen him more than I have. I've talked to him, and he does come over, but he's still cold to me," Jasmine stated.

"Can you blame him? All the bullshit you put him through, and the thing you accuse him of doing, you get caught doing red-handed," Candy said. The anger in her voice took me by surprise. "You know you fucked up, or at least I hope you know you did."

"Okay, Candy, chill," I calmed her down. "Jasmine, what were you thinking?"

"I needed some attention, damn it!" Jasmine yelled. "He gets all the attention when we're out at parties. I wanted to join with him, but these females ain't with it."

"You wonder why?" Candy asked. "You're not sexy. You've got a body, but that's about it."

The whole room got *quiet.*

Candy kept pressing the issue. "This is probably the best I have personally seen you look all year. You say you're bi, but you got them butches at your job gassing your head up like you're the second coming of Pam Grier."

Jasmine had the nerve to look insulted. "I can have anyone I want, once I show my body off. Hell, I've even got you two beat. So how am I not sexy?"

"Because it's your attitude, bitch," I finally chimed in. It's time to set this woman straight on a few things. "Candy's right, you've bought into your own press. You think you're better than everyone else, like it's a privilege to fuck you or something."

"Oh, so it's my fault?" Jasmine huffed. "These people have no game at these parties, Mercedes."

"You just don't get it, do you? Look, Jay is a lot like Kane. He doesn't put on airs or acts like he's better than you. He makes women feel sexy, and they feel at ease around him." I had to lay it all out for her, to make her understand. "All you do is frown at people, making sure no one approaches you. Do you understand that turns people off? I mean, word gets around, Jasmine."

"*I don't give a fuck about those people!*" Jasmine yelled again, this time with tears in her eyes. "*I just want my husband back! These bitches don't hold a candle to me, and he knows that!*"

"Jasmine, you never lost your husband. If you did, he would have beaten your ass, and probably killed the guys you were fucking when you *thought* he was gonna crash at Kane and Mercedes' place that night, like he usually does when you kick him out." Candy had just about reached her boiling point. "He still goes home with you, and manages to fuck your brains out when you get home. I know, because you bragged about it all the time. Do you know how many women would kill to have a man like Jay to be married to?"

"All right, ladies, enough," I finally stated. "Jasmine, after what he caught you doing, I'm honestly surprised Jay even wants to see you right now."

"But..." Jasmine tried to protest.

"But nothing, Jasmine," I cut her off. "You've been blasting your husband for things he never did, kicking him out of the house, embarrassing him at parties; the list goes on, and he still stuck by you. Now, you expect him to forgive and forget, come back home to you so you can have your ego intact? You really have to be living in a dream world."

"Yes. He's my husband. We will get past this. We...we have to," Jasmine flatly answered, as if she were trying to convince herself.

"Then you deserve your fate," I stated. The ice in my stare was unmistakable, and I really wasn't in the mood anymore. "You want to control something, buy a damn dog."

Even Candy took a step back after that comment. I guess my husband rubbed off on me a little more than I cared to admit as well. He usually said things like that, matter-of-factly, and it usually got the point across. By the look on Jasmine's face, I'd say I did a decent job of doing that.

But you know how we women can be.

We had to have the last word.

"I don't control my husband, Mercedes. I let him do whatever he wants to do at parties, let him hang out with his boys. How could you say such a thing?" Jasmine asked.

"Because it's true, you treat him like a child. You want to limit the people he deals with, and they had better be able to live up to your impossible standards. No wonder my husband can't stand you. What's the term he uses to describe you when Jay's over on Poker nights? Oh yeah, 'do you need to check in with the warden?'"

"Mercedes, please, she's had enough." Candy knew I was bringing out the heavy artillery, and she tried desperately to intervene.

"I'm not done," I snapped back at Candy before turning my attention back to Jasmine. "I remember when you tried to confide in us, telling us you don't trust him, and I see now you were the one who shouldn't have been trusted the whole time, and probably should have never been. I know the guys you got with that night, and they both told me *you* came at them, desperate as hell to get back at your husband because you thought he was cheating on you and using Kane to cover for him. So, the way I see it, you're gonna have to damn near kiss his ass and hope he wants to work things out."

"Okay. Okay," was all Jasmine could say. She slumped on the couch, letting the words that I'd just said to her sink in completely. She'd been busted. Like I tried to tell her, the alternative community was a very small, very close-knit one because there are so few of us who do WIITWD, or *what it is that we do*. I guess the prospect of actually losing her husband was enough to actually humble her for a change.

Jasmine walked out on the patio to try and compose herself, and I needed to cool down as well. I sat down at the bar and put my head in my hands, in a desperate attempt to relax my mind, trying to find a peaceful place. Candy placed her hand on my back, checking on me with the hope of finding out what happened to her best friend.

"What got into you, baby? You would have thought Jay was blood or something?" Candy asked.

He wasn't blood, but he is my husband's best friend, which makes him family. Right now, he needed someone in his corner, and for the first time since they were married, I was concerned that that person was no longer Jasmine.

8 ൠ NEFERTERRI

It's been a few weeks since that crazy night, but thankfully things settled down to a crawl. Jay still hadn't gone back to Jasmine, although he did manage to spend a few nights at home for a while.

It wasn't going to be easy, but I had faith things would work themselves out. Blame it on the optimist in me.

But with school around the corner, it was going to be a little more difficult to actually get some "play time" in. Parties happened in waves when it came to this lifestyle. Very rarely was it hot all year, every year.

Candy decided she needed to take a break from hosting at her house, which was fine because no one was planning on doing anything major between now and Amenhotep's party on Halloween. Since the holiday fell on the weekend this year, it's gonna make for one "hell" of a good time. Well, once the kids were done with trick-or-treating of course. Besides, it gave us girls some down time from the summer madness and to do some early costume shopping for the kids. As far as the adults were concerned, the type of shopping for costumes that we wanted to wear couldn't be done in the "regular" stores.

I think we were all stunned when word got out Jay and Jasmine had separated. We still saw them online, and Jay still came over on Poker nights, but no one had really figured out where he had been staying. Even as tight as he and Kane were, not even he knew where he was. Rumors were rampant he was at an ex's house, but nothing was confirmed until I made an unexpected visit over to Candy's house after leaving work early today.

We usually had long lapses where Candy and I kept in touch, but we didn't physically see each other. I had a key to her place, and vice-versa, so, it was nothing to pop up and hang out, and my excuse this time was the aforementioned costume shopping for the kids. But instead of surprising her, imagine my surprise in seeing Jay's bike covered in the garage.

"Well, I'll be damned." I shook my head. I didn't know that those two were even that close to begin with. But then again, there were probably things that even best friends don't always share.

Candy opened the door and acted like she'd seen a ghost. She knew I'd caught her, but the question in her mind was how much did she think I knew?

"Damn, is it five already? So, what are you gonna be for Halloween this year?" Candy asked nonchalantly.

There was no sense in beating around the bush, so I came out and asked, "How long has he been staying here with you?"

Candy acted like she'd been slapped. "Are you gonna hear me out, or are you gonna blast me?"

Well, since she put it that way, I sat down on the couch to hear my girl out. "All right, baby, talk to me, because you know this doesn't look right."

"Jay needed a friend. Someone that he could talk to that wouldn't try to play marriage counselor. He's really confused right now, baby," Candy explained. "He needed to lay low for a while, and he knew my place would be the last place that anyone would look to find him."

"Wait a minute," I responded. "You can't be serious. After the way you lit into Jasmine a few weeks ago, what would make you think she wouldn't think to come by here?"

"Baby, you know Jasmine has been—and would have been—calling over at your house, waking up the kids, looking for him. You know I'm right, Mercedes," Candy said, reading my mind. Everyone knew that Kane and Jay are tight. "And I wasn't the one who ripped her to shreds at my house, Mercedes; you were."

Candy had a point. The last few weeks, Jasmine had been so convinced that Jay was with one of his ex-girlfriends she literally went to the one house where she suspected him to be and confronted the poor woman about it. Last I heard she took a restraining order out on Jasmine to get some peace. After the blowup that we had with her, this would have been the last place Jasmine would think to look. Even if she did, she wouldn't have the guts to take the chance in finding out.

"Okay, so what's going on? You can trust me not to blow the whistle, right?" I asked.

"Jay has been careful not to have Jasmine find out where he is. So, yes, I'm asking you to keep this under wraps for now, baby," Candy replied, and then braced for the impact of the next statement that she was about to make. "Especially considering that we've gotten close over the past few weeks."

"*Close?!?!?!?!*" I yelled. My mind raced, but I tried to keep my promise to stay calm and not blast her. "Okay, what the hell are you thinking?"

Candy sat down next to me. "Jay and I have always been cool. But over the last year, I'd taken notice of how Jasmine mistreats him. Everyone has. So, when all this went down, he naturally gravitated towards me. This wasn't planned, Mercedes, I swear."

I really needed to concentrate, but it wasn't an option at that moment. Candy and I were close, too close for some who were on the outside looking in, but that's their opinion. Right now, my best friend needed me, and I was not turning my back on her. "You know I got your back, baby, if this is what you want to do, but this could get sticky."

"If it will make you feel any better, we haven't slept together, period. Now, I won't lie, I might catch feelings if I'm not careful, but karma's a bitch that I'm not messing with right now," Candy reassured. "Jay and I are friends, for now. Besides, you know that you and Kane are my first option if I need sum, and I know I'm not supposed to do anything without your permission."

I admit, it did feel good to hear her say it, but I also knew that some shit was gonna go down because of the decision my best friend had made.

9 NEFERTERRI

Let's get ready to rumble…

Somehow we were able to get Jay and Jasmine to sit down and talk without yelling a couple of days after I'd found out about Jay's whereabouts. Jasmine was still being stubborn about the whole episode, trying to blame Jay for her cheating on him. I gave her a dirty look when she tried to pull that stunt, and after what I informed him about the two "gentlemen" that were involved in this whole mess, he cut his eyes at her, too. This was a nightmare waiting to happen, but something had to give, and they needed to get things handled, one way or another.

Ramesses had gotten to the point where he needed to stay out of the line of fire and let them work things out, regardless of the outcome. Candy and I joined him to give them some privacy. A few moments later, Jay came outside to get some air. He looked exhausted.

"You cool?" Ramesses asked him.

"Just memories, that's all. Things have changed. Can't live off the past," he replied. He put his head in his hands. He needed to hear himself saying the words.

"It doesn't have to change, dawg. I know what she did was fucked up, but you've had time to cool off from it, right?" Don't ask me why he was playing Dr. Phil at that point, but he wanted to do something to keep his partner from hurting so bad.

"Look, K, I know I've told you before, you're like a brother to me, but after what Jasmine did to me." He felt himself getting upset all over again, but then calmed down to ice-cold calmness. "It's over, Kane."

"What the...?" He wanted to ask why, among other things, but Jay beat us to it.

"There is no one else, if that's what you're thinking. When I sat down to think, I realized Jasmine never loved me. She loved the control that she had over me. When we jumped into this lifestyle, her rules were restrictive, to say the least, until she got with you when we were at your birthday party," he said to me. "Then the rules changed for her, but she still had to see what I was up to at all times. When the women weren't feeling her vibe, her control over me started to slip, especially after Candy cussed her out at one of her house parties."

It became clear to me. Jay was tired of being put in "time out" every time "mommy" was mad at him. Meanwhile, mommy was out playing and breaking the very rules that she was trying to hold him to, while using the time-honored parental cop-out of, "do as I say, not as I do."

Shit got thick real quick, and it was only a matter of time before it got worse once we headed back into the house.

I can't remember the last time I saw a man so cold.

Jay sat there stone-faced while Jasmine tried her best to get him pissed enough to yell back at her. No matter what she said, it didn't faze him one bit. He had me really worried.

"Are you done, Jasmine?" Jay calmly asked her. "I need to speak my peace now."

His demeanor was stoic, even Jasmine had to pause. She watched him move with a purpose across the room, closing in on her to make sure his point resonated within her.

"You know, I was upset enough to do something really stupid that night," he said. "But I probably would not be a free man right now if I did."

"Please, Jay, spare me the—"

"Did I say I was finished?!?!" Jay snapped, which really shut Jasmine down. Out of the corner of my eye, I saw Candy smirk, enjoying the show. Meanwhile, I saw a man who, in the course of a day, had finally found his balance again.

"You have no control anymore. You lost that when you got caught cheating." His eyes got small, almost piercing through Jasmine as he said it. It looked like he was exorcising a ghost from his body and mind. "I'm sorry I ever gave you that power over me."

"It was just one night, baby." Jasmine was in panic mode, and it was beginning to show. "You're not gonna throw away what we have over that, are you? I'll do whatever you want, please???" She sounded defeatist, like she wasn't sure if she would be able to persuade him this time.

"Here's what's funny, baby. If you had said that instead of blaming me for all of this, I would have probably believed you. That's how much I loved you," Jay pointed out. "But instead, you decided it was better to insult me; put the blame on me to make yourself feel better."

Being a student of power exchange, you could tell when someone was losing their power and energy over someone else. Jasmine's color began to fade to pale as she began to realize her marriage was coming to an end.

"Please, honey, please don't do this. I love you, we can work this out." Jasmine was in full panic mode now, begging Jay to reconsider, but Jay wasn't having it.

"My lawyer will be in contact next week. I want a divorce, Jasmine." Jay finally breathed the words he thought he would never have to say. "You can have the house, because I can't live here anymore."

"No!" Jasmine yelled. *"You can't leave me. Your place is here, damn it!"*

"Not anymore, Jasmine." Jay never raised his voice, not once. "Not anymore."

Jasmine collapsed in tears on the couch. Jay just stood there, and Ramesses said to him,

"Dawg, it's time to roll. There's nothing more left to say."

"All of you can go to hell!" Jasmine yelled after us. *"I'll make you all pay for what you did to me!"*

Once we got outside, Jay softly uttered, "I didn't deserve her anyway." His energy was spent, and it looked like he had been through his own personal hell to get to this point. There was still love in his eyes, and pain as well. It was a look I would never wish upon my worst enemy, and one that I prayed I would never have to go through with my husband.

Candy corrected him quickly. "No, she didn't deserve you." She kissed him to make her point clearer.

The look on Kane's face, to let me tell it, was one of a kind. "Never jump without a parachute, huh, bro?" he mentioned.

"You taught me well, bro," Jay replied before getting back on his bike. "I'm just making sure that I don't get caught out there like that again."

☥

Once word got around about Jay and Jasmine, my phone would not stop ringing.

The women ripped Jasmine to shreds for days, and in the same breath, wondered where they could find Jay to make him "feel better." It got so widespread, even Amenhotep called to confirm things. All Ramesses could do was to deflect the attention as much as he could.

Speaking of getting heads together, it led him to his next head-scratching moment: Candy acting more than just a "friend" last week. "What in the hell was she thinking," he kept saying. Without proof of her infidelity, Jay could get screwed in court. Things would get really complicated if he didn't keep his manhood in check. Jasmine was not one to just lie down and take it. He had a point, and I knew it.

To take his mind off things, he decided that a ride would do him some good, so, he pulled his bike out of the back area where he and I kept them. That's when we noticed someone in a car across the street watching us. I couldn't tell the type, but it was a dark-red sedan.

I didn't give myself away. I knew the person was watching, and he made sure to keep doing what he was doing so that they wouldn't get too spooked.

"You're not getting away that easily," he said as he walked back in the house to get his camera. When he came back out, he faked as if he were taking pictures of me on the bike, using the zoom lens to get a good look at who might be having beef with us. The lens got a good look at the plate number as the car sped away.

"Never fuck with a cop's family, dumb ass," he said as he wrote the number down from the digital image. The only thing I hoped was they didn't use bogus plates.

10 ∞ RAMESSES

"So, what's on for tonight, dawg?"

Jay seemed to be completely over what had happened to him a couple of weeks ago. It was as if he were trying hard to forget that any of it ever had happened. "Are you meeting us at the spot or what?"

I was a bit concerned he was being so cavalier about his impending divorce, but he was intent on making a clean break, even giving up the house in the divorce settlement. I guess he really wanted no reminders of Jasmine. But then again, I didn't know what he was going through, considering I'm not a big proponent of monogamy.

I took a look at my watch, which read around six, and hoped Neferterri would be ready to roll by the time I got home. She always liked making a grand entrance, but I hated being late. "Yeah, we should be there by eight or so. I'm just leaving the job now."

"Cool, Kane, we'll be in the VIP as usual," Jay stated.

It was like that every Friday night of the month, when we headed to the club that my wife partly owns: Liquid Paradise, or Liquid, for short. We usually hang out with some of the newbies we chat with online or become new to the online group we run, and then head either to Candy's or down to our house for an impromptu after-party.

I took the long way home, even though I knew it might make

us a little late. Oh well, can't be on time all the damn time. But it gave me an opportunity to reflect back on a few things that had occurred recently.

In some cases, I guess my life has been pretty full. I have a beautiful, wonderful wife and three hyper-ass-but-well-behaved children. Thanks to some lucky and wise investments, including the club, we are able to stay comfortable in the neighborhood that we live in. We made sure to buy a lot with at least one acre on it, to make sure the neighbors didn't get too nosey.

As far as things outside of our personal "vanilla" lives are concerned, I guess we're as close to celebrities as you can get. Neferterri and Candy are models for a website called "Full Figgaz," which I was proud about, especially when I had a hand in the initial photographs being sent to the company. Hey, having camera skills is a player's best asset, and it did wonders for finding, and breaking in, potential females curious about the lifestyle.

But, I couldn't get my mind away from the other stuff that had popped up in recent weeks: the bullshit with Jasmine; the person in the car that insisted on spying on me at my house; Jay acting like he was never married to begin with. It was beginning to weigh on me, and I couldn't let that happen. Besides, I'm happily married, even as a libertine, I'm happily married. Neferterri and I have a strong foundation, regardless of what it is that we do. Without that foundation, the alternative lifestyle can tear you up and spit you out.

Unfortunately, Jay and Jasmine found out the hard way.

I finally pulled into the driveway, checking the grass to make sure that it didn't need to be cut. Damn HOAs, I swear they can work your nerves sometimes. Once I got the car in the garage, I got out and headed into the house to see about Neferterri.

"Hey, babe, you ready to go?" I was relieved to find her putting the finishing touches on her outfit.

"Hey, sexy, just waiting on you," she replied as she gave me a quick peck on the lips. "shamise said she'll meet us at the club, but jamii and nuru can't make it."

I sort of bypassed that statement as I quickly jumped in the shower, mainly because I really wasn't in the mood to bother with them. I would have to deal with them sooner or later, though. There was nothing worse than a submissive who really insisted on acting a fool for no reason. If they thought that this was a good way to get attention, they both had another thing coming.

On the bed, I saw she already had the outfit she wanted me in set out on the bed. Don't get the wrong idea; I can dress myself, but I was in a rush, and my wife knows what I like to wear.

Once I got out of the shower, I saw Mercedes talking to some dude online who allowed her to view his webcam. I took a look at his screen name, which read "da_greatest." Yeah, I know. I laughed when I saw it, too.

"Who's this, someone wanting to take you from me as usual?" I joked.

"Nope, even better, baby. He claims he would be the greatest sex I or any of my girls will ever have. Never mind that I am a happily married woman, because he can change all that." Mercedes giggled. She'd heard that line before. In most cases, they never are able to "rise" to the occasion.

The man must have lost his mind at some point during the conversation, because he asked a question that most single men have no business asking a married woman:

da_greatest: *so when can I come over so we can do this?*

daddys_mercedes: *you really are stupid…only at parties*

da_greatest: *yeah, I know, but I know I could make your toes curl if we had some private time*

daddys_mercedes: *no deal. only way you see me at all is at Liquid tonight, and if you're a good boy, then we'll go from there*

da_greatest: *damn girl, you drive a hard bargain. see you tonight. How will I know who you are?*

daddys_mercedes: *come to the VIP, you'll see me there. I'll be the one in black sitting with my HUSBAND, with a dancer in my lap giving me some personal attention*

Now by this point, I would have normally taken over the keyboard and said some things to throw ol' boy off a little.

But that was the old me.

"Whatever, dude." Neferterri got up from the PC with a dismissive tone in her voice. I guessed we would probably not see "da greatest" after all.

I rubbed her shoulders gently and reminded her, "Baby, don't sweat it. Besides, you look like you could use a few lap dances tonight before the real fun begins."

☥

We finally got to Liquid and I could tell already it was going to be a long night. There were guys arguing with the bouncers at the door. Not that I worried too much about that. Being me does have its privileges.

"Hey, boys, how are things tonight? I hope these guys aren't giving you too much trouble?" Neferterri said as she walked with me toward the front door. We almost made it inside, when we heard a snap from out of the blue that was meant for my wife to hear.

"Come on, what makes that bitch so special that she gets to get in and we don't?" I heard the little dude in the group have the nerve to say.

I felt the heat rise within me. There were no other women in the immediate vicinity, so there was no doubt the dude with the big mouth was about to have it shut for him. I was ready to let off a few punches, if the security at the door didn't take up for her first.

"So, she's a bitch now, right?" I interjected before my wife got a chance to. "Exactly what has she done to you to make you call her out of her name, especially in front of her husband?"

He saw me make a move on him, and at first, he looked like he was ready to jump and make this night a little more interesting. But once he saw the bouncers weren't trying to stop me, the little dude started thinking twice about the way he spoke.

He started backtracking his words when he saw me getting closer.

Under normal circumstances, I would have simply walked into his personal space, big dude to little dude, and let my presence speak for itself as a cautionary tale. But this time, I needed to pop off a little bit of a personal touch, to make things clear.

"So, are we sorry that we spoke out of line for no reason, or is there going to be a need for violence tonight?" I warned. "I had planned to enjoy the evening with my wife, but she is aware that sometimes business needs to be handled first."

His eyes got big as he apologized. "My bad, dawg, I'm sorry; I didn't mean to disrespect your wife like that. But these security dudes been saying this is a private party, and I'm saying, Mercedes invited us here tonight, but they ain't trying to hear what I'm saying right now."

I saw this disgusted look pop across Mercedes' face the minute he said that, and I knew in an instant that it was the dude that she was chatting with earlier in the evening.

Damn.

He obviously figured it out, too, because his whole attitude changed. "Damn, I guess I should have thought before I opened my big mouth. I really am sorry, Mercedes, I wasn't thinking straight. My boys and I wanted to do this party bad tonight."

Neferterri wasn't impressed by the pseudo-apology. She went into business mode really quick, and I could already tell she was not going to be in the mood to even bother with him once he got in the club. "Well, it's not gonna cut it, shorty. To get in my spot tonight, it's gonna cost you and your boys fifty apiece for the cover, a hundred for the VIP, and every dancer that I send in your direction gets a three dance minimum at twenty a pop. Now, I'm hoping that will teach you not to disrespect a lady, and consider it me letting you off easy, especially when you brought some dudes I didn't approve for you to bring with you."

You figure that after you'd been punked by a woman, and in front of your boys, and your boys had to suffer for your mouth, too, that it would humble you a bit?

Not this dude.

He got this look in his eye, and a grin popped up across his lips, and he straightened himself before stating foolishly, "Aiight, I'll do it, but I get to holla at you once I get inside, right?"

The bouncers felt me flinch, and they could tell I was about at wit's end, so they flanked dude and stood between me and him. I felt the heat rising again, this time to a boiling point, and to be honest, I really was about to exert my "silent partner" privileges at that very moment. I really was not about to be lowered to his level, but it was about two more words to be said before I remembered I still had a little street left in me.

Neferterri didn't flinch. "Okay, since you don't get it, let's make it a hundred on the barrel head, you and your boys, right now, half a grand for the privilege of being in the VIP with me, and if that doesn't shut you up, I don't know what will."

My wife could be cutthroat, especially when she's pissed.

I saw his boys getting a little bit upset, and from the wedding rings on their fingers, I was sure their respective wives would not appreciate a grand being gone from the bank account over foolishness. If I knew my wife, I already knew her money-makers were going to milk them dry.

The tall one on the little dude's right side started twisting his wedding band over and over again, making the calculations in his mind and shaking his head at the end result because he already knew it wasn't gonna happen. The stocky one on the little dude's left side started balling up his fists like his evening had just been ruined, all because of an ego trip and the fact his boy just got punked for not keeping his mouth shut. He looked at me, then looked at Neferterri, and then gave a shrug because he wasn't about to go home with less money than he originally planned to spend either.

"Yo, Lee, let it go, dawg. I ain't getting booted out of the house over your dumb ass," the tall dude mentioned.

"Yeah, man, all this for a party? This shit ain't worth it," the stocky one chirped. "I got better things to do tonight, and she already said she wasn't even expecting us to roll with you, too? Damn, man, appreciate the embarrassment."

"Man, fuck you pussy-whipped muhfuckas. That's why I'm glad I'm single; I get more ass than ya'll do anyway." Lee stomped off, giving me a wild-eyed look.

He was lucky I didn't strap up tonight.

I followed them with my eyes as they all walked to their cars, and I also saw Lee head back in a rush to get to his car…

Of particular interest were the make and color…the same make and color of the car that was at my house.

11 RAMESSES

Being married to a club owner does have its perks.

But it's nothing we broadcast. It causes too many problems on too many levels, and I usually don't tell people on the net unless they happen to be at the club. We both enjoyed being the "silent" partners, while her cousin DeAngelo and his wife, Honey, handled the day-to-day operations. We invested into the club about six months into the operation, and she kept the books.

We did our normal P.R. thing: checking on the girls to make sure that they were getting money and not being mistreated; talking to the house mother as well; and my personal favorite, getting shots from the shot girls before heading up to DeAngelo's office. Man, getting a shot from a shot girl is one of the most erotic things anyone can experience, and it's not a bad way to get tipsy, either.

"Sup, cousin?" DeAngelo greeted as we walked through the door. "I see it's that time of the month as usual."

Neferterri replied, "Looks like business is booming, D. All the underground marketing paid off, after all."

"Shit, that really did the trick. Word of mouth got around quick," he mentioned, looking in my direction. "What's up, Big Game Kane?"

"Man, keep that to yourself, D." I got that nickname back in high school, for my actions both on and off the court.

"Hey, it's not my fault you catching more seafood than Red Lobster can dish out at dinner on a Saturday night." DeAngelo was always corny with the jokes, but that's cool, too. I mean, he is family.

We headed out of his office and back out on the floor in the direction of the VIP area. It was buck-wild as usual, but that's what the area was there for. Besides, if you've been inside of a strip club before, you know the business. If you haven't, it's your loss.

Mercedes walked ahead of me to go find Candy while I kept checking the couples who made it out. I found one Ice was chatting with, so I walked over in their direction to be nosey and see what I could find out about them.

"Kane, you can talk to your boy in a minute; I get to have my attention first, dammit!" I heard Candy shouting over the music at me.

"Damn, you just had to call me out in the VIP, huh?" I asked as I gave my usual suffocating hug to her. "You insisted on having Daddy's attention first, right?"

"Yep." she answered without hesitation. That's my girl.

I turned around and saw my wife in an exchange with some chick who I vaguely remembered. She reminded me of one of the Pussycat Dolls, not the lead singer, but one of the other girls. She was cute as hell, but from my wife's facial expressions, it looked like she and her date were not going to make it to the house tonight.

I looked around for Ice, and I saw the male of the couple had left. It was only she and Ice getting pretty well acquainted and close.

I shook my head, grinning at the sight.

If she only knew what was about to happen to her later on tonight.

As I walked with Candy in Neferterri's direction, I asked, "So where's my surprise? I know she's around here somewhere, and don't be holding out on a brother."

Neferterri winked at Candy, which tipped me off to know someone was standing behind me. I turned around and my mouth *dropped* at the sight of a six-foot Amazon princess standing in my personal space.

"I heard someone was looking for me? Something about being a surprise for this sexy-ass man standing in front of me right now."

From her accent, it was easy to tell she was of Latin descent, I guessed Puerto Rican. "Oh, so you're gonna be keeping me company while my girls are busy?" I looked from head to toe, and thought to myself, *yeah, like I'm gonna complain.*

"*Si, papi,*" she replied, nearly triggering my Dominant side. Damn, why is it always so erotic to hear those words from a woman in Spanish?

"May I have the pleasure of knowing your name, love?" I tried my best, but every time I looked into her eyes, she bowed her head and cast her eyes to the floor. I should have known Candy was gonna say something to her about my "dark" side. But then again, she knows me better than anyone, except Mercedes.

"This girl's name is Angel, Sir." Her voice was softer, more sensual now, so I had to get closer to her to hear what she was saying to me. "It is my honor to serve You and obey Your every command, Sir."

I was not up to summoning the energy it took to be Ramesses tonight, so, I responded by grabbing her by the nape of her neck and whispering, "you will obey My every command, and that doesn't just include tonight, little one."

Angel shuddered, telling me everything I needed to know. But I also knew I needed to slow down on the acquisitions or I'd wear myself out, or even worse, I may have needed to pull an imitation of Amenhotep and include them all under one domicile. But that's not possible, so, I needed to do a re-count and see what needed to happen from here on out.

☥

The way we'd been doing the after-parties had been successful so far.

Each invitee gets a "pass" discreetly placed in their hands, which they will show once they reach the location. The location changes from month to month, so that no one can show up unannounced. They are under strict instruction not to speak to anyone about whether they received the pass or not, otherwise they are denied access, period. I'm even anal enough to send out "moles" to make sure the rules are being followed. The guests are expected to be at the location by midnight, or they were expected to give a "donation" for the inconvenience of being late. Like I said: my party, MY rules. Once you're there, the rest comes naturally.

I found Ice and Jay chilling on the couch, with Kitana nowhere in sight. Come to think of it, neither was shamise, and I usually kept up with where my girls were at all times, including my wife. Then it hit me: they're all in one of the master suites doing their "all girl hour."

Damn it.

"Yeah, you remembered what time it is, too, huh, K?" Jay asked, looking depressed. "Why is it all the fine, sexy-ass ones are always bi?"

Ice nodded in agreement. "I was hoping to get at Angel before they went in, but nope. Your wife made me come back down here to think about where my loyalties are, and to whom I belong."

Leave it to Neferterri to do what she did best. But what had me confused was why they would put Angel in front of me, only to keep me waiting until they get done with her?

The answer to my thoughts came in the form of Neferterri walking toward me, with both Kitana and Angel on collars and leashes, leading them to me. They were both crawling on their hands and knees, which caught the attention of every other man in the room.

She stopped long enough to give me the leashes, before she stated, "These girls belong to You now, Beloved; do with them as You wish."

Neferterri then turned to Ice and harshly commanded, "your Mistress wishes to see you now, slave. Move!"

If you've never seen a man so completely humiliated, then you would have been in for one special treat. Ice's face went from delight to pure dread in a matter of seconds, not only from being dropped into sub mode, but also because it was done in front of his wife as well. Add his punishment for what he did, or didn't do, at Amenhotep's a month ago, was long overdue from his Mistress, and he had more than enough reasons to look like a dead man walking.

But it didn't stop me from reminding myself that I had two submissive females at my feet, and one of my boys who was in need of attention.

I turned the leash that belonged to Kitana over to Jay, who was drooling at the sight of her being butt naked on all fours.

"Have fun, bro…but not too much fun. she will report back to Me if you do something you weren't supposed to," I told him before I led Angel away on her leash.

I said it before, but it bears repeating…

I *loved* my lifestyle.

12 ⊛ RAMESSES

I needed a couple of days rest after that club event and after-party.

Thankfully with October arriving, business was starting to slow down, allowing me to take a quick breather before starting the Christmas holiday season. It was some much needed time to recharge the old batteries and to try and take stock of what had transpired over the summer.

I know sometimes it's not fair to say it, but the laws of attraction usually applied a lot within this lifestyle, and whether intentional or not, some attractions are stronger than others. The electricity Kitana and I had was dangerously explosive when we got together. Everyone who witnessed the flogging session she and I had after Jay turned her back over to me later on that night was something absolutely euphoric for me.

With each instrument of painful pleasure I chose to use on Kitana, her body spoke to me to keep bringing the thunder. It was a yin-yang moment, the blend of give and take that doesn't happen often. In fact, I've only experienced this fluidity with only one of our girls, and that was shamise. It didn't matter what I picked up, it seemed to send Kitana's body into a rhythmic dance, enhanced by the scene music I chose only for her flogging sessions.

Now, don't get me wrong. I've made sure each of our girls has her own particular song within the scene music selection that helps to open her mind, and her body to soon follow, to the sweet rapture of subspace. But tonight, it felt different. Kitana was determined to prove she belonged with the other girls in the House, and the song she chose to bring her over the edge was "Say Yes" by Floetry. Her body sang out "yes" with every swing and stinging impact upon her skin.

Damn. Even thinking of it now was sending shivers down my spine.

Her ears must have been burning or something, because at that exact moment, the IM I'd created for her popped up on my computer screen.

hypnotiq_kitana: *Good morning, my Sir. i hope Your morning is going well*

lord_ramesses: *Good morning, sexy…and how are you this morning?*

hypnotiq_kitana: *i am well, my Sir. i was just thinking about You and my Goddess*

hypnotiq_kitana: *Sir...may i ask a personal question?*

lord_ramesses: *yes you may*

hypnotiq_kitana: *how much experience do You have with knife play?*

lord_ramesses: *give or take...about three years now...*

lord_ramesses: *I have a personal knife collection*

lord_ramesses: *plus, Neferterri enjoys it a lot too...*

lord_ramesses: *that's what got Me deep into it*

hypnotiq_kitana: *wow Sir, impressive*

lord_ramesses: *yep...*

lord_ramesses: *I've fallen in love with it now*

lord_ramesses: *My next step is actually using sharper knives*

lord_ramesses: *rather than dulling them down*

hypnotiq_kitana: *so are You into actually cutting now?*

lord_ramesses: *not cutting, no, little one*

lord_ramesses: *not into blood games, so no worries there lol*

hypnotiq_kitana: *Whew...good to know*

lord_ramesses: *lol...*

lord_ramesses: *no blood...no water sports either*

I knew from the questions she asked, Kitana had been doing a lot of reading online and going into information overload. It was cute to see, and gave me a fresh pair of eyes on something I'd been living for so long, it was actually getting my own creative passions back in gear.

hypnotiq_kitana: *i'm loving You more and more...lol*

lord_ramesses: *lol...*

hypnotiq_kitana: *what about fire play or cupping*

lord_ramesses: *haven't found a willing participant for the fire play*

lord_ramesses: *and we have a cupping set in the bag, as we speak*

hypnotiq_kitana: *i'm volunteering for both*

lord_ramesses: *loving you already*

hypnotiq_kitana: *lol*

lord_ramesses: *every sub that I have spoken to before you…even Our girls…they cringe before I can type the f-i in fire play*

hypnotiq_kitana: *well, Sir, i'm starting to develop a lot of curiosities, and i want to try as much as You and Goddess will allow me to*

lord_ramesses: *good girl…I like that*

I guess I was predisposed to wanting Kitana as more than a swinging partner from time to time. In my mind, it was never about the conquest. At least I didn't think it was. There was a deeper friendship that had always been there, and outside of Neferterri, she's the only one who understood my mind and quirks. Yeah, I know, it sounded selfish as hell, but I'm not perfect by any stretch of the imagination.

In the grand scheme of what this House represented, all of the submissives within this House understood one simple point: this was a Poly family dynamic, which meant there really was no time for extended one-on-one time. I kept that upfront and in the forefront of their minds periodically. But I had to be prepared, as my Beloved was as well, for the inevitability that one or all of the girls would decide they no longer wished to belong within this House. It's not a pleasant thought, but reality was a bitch sometimes.

I kept asking different questions of Kitana, to see whether she really was as committed as we'd already figured from that night at safi's collaring.

lord_ramesses: *do you understand that this is what we are? This isn't a game, baby. We've been friends too long, and this is another level entirely*

hypnotiq_kitana: *may i speak freely, Sir?*

lord_ramesses: *go ahead*

hypnotiq_kitana: *Sir, i never told You this, but i have been speaking with other submissives online…ones that I saw that held you in high regard, and i asked their advice and asked questions whenever I got stuck with something*

lord_ramesses: *so I see…so you already knew you were ready before you pulled your move that night at Amenhotep's?*

hypnotiq_kitana: **blushes* i almost didn't do it, my Sir…but i couldn't leave that night without finding out how deep this could go*

lord_ramesses: *and now that you have an idea, was it everything that your mind built it up to be?*

hypnotiq_kitana: *yes, and i am scared and excited as to what is to come next*

The beauty of a blank canvas…

13 ∞ RAMESSES

"Ms. Devereaux? There is a gentleman and his associate here to see you, ma'am."

Candy had no idea of what was about to happen to her, especially considering it was the middle of the day and she thought her assistant referred to the person she was supposed to be negotiating a business deal with. She'd been working on this deal for weeks, and she wanted to make a good impression.

"Send them in, Jessica," Candy responded through the intercom to her executive assistant. "Hold my calls for at least the next hour, please."

"Yes, ma'am." Jessica's voice rang through the intercom.

Candy was a top-level ad executive for a big-time marketing firm in downtown Atlanta. Her responsibilities had been recently escalated to handling the company's European clientele. The person she was expecting was flying in from London to broker in person a deal to have the firm represent them in a rather "underground" project they were undertaking in London's Red Light District.

She was pleasantly shocked to see Neferterri and me walking through the door in business attire. Shocked, and confused.

"What are you two doing here?" she asked as Jessica closed the door after seeing us into her office. What Candy didn't see was the knowing wink I gave to Jessica to bring in the Euro client at the proper time. If she played her cards right, it could be a very interesting sight to participate in.

"Don't worry about all that, baby. I see you wore the corset and skirt I told you to wear for your client...good girl," Neferterri stated, letting her eyes scan from the pony tail Candy wore to the all-leather halter corset and matching leather skirt, all the way down to the ankle-length leather boots that accentuated her legs. "Doesn't she look wonderful, Daddy?"

"Yes, she does indeed." I stepped closer to Candy, inhaling the perfume she knew I loved on her. "I wonder if she made sure not to wear any panties."

Candy was mesmerized by the way things started to transpire. "Yes, Daddy, just like you commanded last night, and your pussy is bare as well."

"Show me."

Candy hesitated for a moment. "My European client will be here at any moment, Daddy."

"You're saying that as if I care?" I responded, forcefully moving her to the edge of her desk and pulling her skirt up so I could find out for myself. "Mmmm, good girl, you're nice and bare, and slick as well. Is that for your client to notice?"

"My client is female, and I have been getting some vibes from her that she might want to—"

"Fuck you...like I'm planning to right now, baby." Neferterri finished Candy's comment. As she answered, she unbuttoned her pants to reveal a rather interesting surprise that made Candy lick her lips and grin so hard her cheeks began to hurt.

"Is that what I think that is?"

"Yes, it is, baby."

What Candy was referring to was a *FeelDoe* strap-on dildo hidden under Neferterri's business suit.

For those who might not understand, allow me to explain:

If you've watched porn videos before, then you know that the strap-on devices that are used in some of them are rather flimsy to say the least. The FeelDoe is made in such a manner that it contours into the vaginal canal, thick enough to fill the canal entirely, and rests right at the G-spot, which allows its female wearer the ability to literally feel the penetration, to give her the sensation of what a man feels when he is penetrating a woman.

Key words: *mutual satisfaction.*

You gotta love the lesbians who made this device...I know my Beloved does.

I moved out of the way and allowed Neferterri to spread Candy's legs apart while she was still on the desk. The minute the head found its way inside of her wetness, Candy let out a satisfied moan like it was exactly what the sex doctor ordered.

"Oh my God, that feels *soooo* good." I saw the lust in Candy's eyes as she caressed Neferterri through the fabric of the pants.

Neferterri pulled Candy's leg and rested it over her shoulder and slowly slid deeper inside, breathing deeper as she began to stroke. They shared deep, sensual kisses as she stroked, almost forgetting I was in the room for a moment. I smiled and took the moment to slip out of the room and let them really get into it. My phone vibrated, letting me know the client Candy was waiting for had arrived.

I met Jessica in the reception area, taking notice of the stunning woman waiting for me. I stopped for a moment to take in her essence, enjoying the sight before I spoke.

"Good afternoon, Ms. Devereaux is showing you her presentation as soon as you walk in the door, Ms. ...?"

"Jameson, Sir. Lillian Jameson. I'm pleased to make your acquaintance." She presented her hand to me and I properly gave her a kiss on the back of her palm. "My, I'm in the presence of a gentleman as well. It's such a rare commodity these days."

I knew she would melt when I did that. The British women are suckers for gentlemanly and chivalrous behavior, even in the twenty-first century. She was a very statuesque woman, perhaps late thirties or so, very voluptuous figure, not too top heavy, maybe a C-cup at the least, but a beauty nonetheless. She wore a conservative, knee-length pencil skirt, stiletto heels, and a black blouse and jacket. She dressed in a manner as to not draw too much attention to herself, but I had a feeling the conservative attire hid something more sensual beneath. This was going to be an interesting meeting after all, one that might take a little more than the hour than Candy originally anticipated. The choker/collar around her neck provided the information I needed, and provide the necessary confidence the scene in front of her would produce the desired results. Thank goodness Jessica was in the know as well. She should have been, as she's one of Amenhotep's service slaves allowed to work outside of the Palace.

Ms. Jameson wouldn't be in a tremendous shock when we opened that door, but I buttered her up. I had a feeling I was going to need to take care of some business in a few moments. I wanted her at ease to be able to help Candy finish the presentation on a high note with closing the deal.

Upon seeing the choker around Ms. Jameson's neck, I asked her bluntly, "Does your Master know what you are undertaking?"

She lowered her head as she replied, "Yes, Sir, my Master is aware. I am acting on His behalf and Ms. Devereaux came highly recommended for her ability to be discreet."

Now this had some potential indeed. I had a feeling I might need to make a trip over to London in the near future to see about some things. It might prove beneficial for all involved.

"Well, Ms. Jameson, I believe you will enjoy what you're about to see. The sensuality you asked for your campaign is occurring as we are speaking. Come, let me show you."

Jessica led the way, no doubt preparing herself for the scene she also would witness. We slipped inside as not to allow the passionate moans and screams to escape from the office. What Ms. Jameson saw was quite lovely indeed.

Neferterri and Candy were on the couch in the office, going at it doggie style now. Candy's breasts were now released from the corset and her skirt was hiked up over her ass as my wife was rhythmically stroking her, switching from a steady pace to something more primal, more urgent, pushing Candy to come and come hard.

"Oh my," Ms. Jameson whispered. "They look absolutely beautiful together."

Watching the lustful looks on my girls, I flashed a proud grin. They didn't notice us entering the room, which had been my intent for Ms. Jameson to catch the natural essence of the presentation.

I felt Ms. Jameson lean against me, her hand unconsciously tracing the lining of her bra. Her head began to tilt back against my chest, and I instinctively moved my hands down to her waist to steady her, allowing her to soak in the entire scene.

Jessica tapped me on the shoulder and whispered into my ear, "Shall I tell the partners that Ms. Devereaux will need two hours and the contract will be signed and delivered, yes, Sir?"

"Yes, Jessica, you can tell the partners it will be signed in the morning."

Jessica tipped out of the office to relay the message while I continued buttering up Ms. Jameson for the close.

"Ms. Devereaux knows her clientele and what they need to present the proper image, Ms. Jameson."

"Yes, she does indeed, Sir...may i call You Sir?"

"you may refer to Me as Lord Ramesses, My dear."

"my Master will be pleased to know His project will be in capable hands from a marketing standpoint, m'Lord."

"I assure you it is in good hands, just as you are in Mine, Ms. Jameson."

"Mmmm, indeed i am m'Lord, if i am allowed to say so."

I moved my hands from her waist to the buttons on her blouse, slowly unbuttoning them and exposing the lace bra underneath. A soft moan escaped her lips, and she covered my hands with hers to continue to unfasten the rest of her blouse, exposing her tanned skin.

"Take your breasts out of your bra, Ms. Jameson. I'm sure they need some attention, considering the beautiful scene in front of you."

She did as ordered, unclasping the hook between her breasts, gasping at her exposed breasts and hardened nipples that were now being pinched and teased by her fingers.

"This has to be one of the most erotic presentations that I've been a part of, m'Lord." She whispered again, this time too aroused to speak above that whisper. "If they keep this up, I might need to call and ask permission from my Master to release some tension."

I soon heard the sweet sounds of Candy's orgasm, and Neferterri realized we were in the room with them and had been the entire time. She looked at the position I had Ms. Jameson in and knew the deal was closed.

Candy was still in the throes of her orgasm, cursing a few deities along the journey to the epicenter of her pleasure. She collapsed on the couch, trying desperately to slow her breathing, knowing she needed to be prepared for her client that she knew had to be...

"Ahem. Looks like I found the proper ad exec to fuel my campaign," Ms. Jameson stated, blushing slightly upon witnessing the final sensual moments between Neferterri and Candy. She tried to compose herself from allowing me to expose her chest and fondle her while she enjoyed the show.

"Ms. Jameson...I'm sorry, I had prepared for your arrival, but..." Candy panicked, thinking the deal was blown, but she quickly realized her client was half naked as well.

"No need to apologize, Ms. Devereaux. Your lovers seemed to have helped you close the deal on this marketing campaign. I will let my employer know that the contract is yours."

"Thank you, Ms. Jameson. I will get the contract over to your lawyers in the morning," Candy ecstatically stated as she was trying to dress herself. Mercedes was sitting on the couch reapplying her makeup and freshening up as well.

"I'm sure there's no need to get dressed just yet, Ms. Devereaux. I was hoping you would make sure the deal was sealed by doing to me what your lover has just done to you?" Ms. Jameson grinned, breaking from my grasp to fondle Candy's breasts as well.

"Well, I believe these negotiations are just getting started, baby. Besides, we have a bit of business to attend to also," Neferterri said rhetorically as we headed out of the office to leave the ladies to finish their "negotiations" in private. "Oh, and please make sure Ms. Devereaux gives you our numbers as well. Enjoy the rest of your negotiations."

14 RAMESSES

Kneeling on the floor naked, she was intensely aware of everything around her.

The business we needed to attend to after we left Candy's office was to take care of the inspection phase of Kitana's training with us. Not two hours after taking care of Candy and her client, Kitana was naked in our living room, making sure this phase of her awakening had been completed. The kids were at their grandparents' house, so we wouldn't be disturbed for a few hours.

Every sound, every smell seemed magnified around her. I could hear her breathing and felt her heart pounding as I pressed my hand against her chest. She heard me moving across the room toward her and instinctively she lifted her head, her eyes meeting my gaze.

"Did I tell you to look at Me?" I snapped.

My voice was level and its tone was inquiring, more than annoyed. This was the side of me that Kitana needed to see; the stern, unyielding force who demanded House protocol be executed. She needed to see this from the both of us, to let her know that while there is pleasure in this journey, there is also transgression and punishment as well.

She lowered her eyes, feeling a shiver of apprehension race up her spine as she whispered, "i'm sorry, m'Lord. i forgot myself; please forgive me."

"Forgiveness is not an option here," I said as my fingers twisted into the silkiness of her hair. "you have broken protocol and you must learn that is not acceptable."

"Yes, m'Lord."

I walked slowly around Kitana, ensuring her eyes were still cast downward.

Neferterri sat in a chair in the living room, observing the entire interaction. She picked up her cell phone, pressed a key, and within a couple of seconds she was on the phone speaking. I couldn't make out who she was speaking with; I concentrated on Kitana.

"you are our property and as such we expect total obedience." I paused, almost for effect, before I asked, "So what do you think should happen now?"

Nervously, she licked her lips knowing the moment she had been anticipating was near. Her voice quivered slightly as she uttered, "You must punish me, m'Lord, in whatever way You see fit."

"Indeed I must punish you and I intend to do so in many and varied ways. Some, no doubt, you will enjoy; others you will not." I repeated her words so that she could feel the full effect of her words. "By the end of today, we will see tears flowing freely down your cheeks. You will learn your pleasure is in our hands, to mete out as and when either of us sees fit. Now, have you chosen your safe word yet?" I questioned. "It is essential before we begin."

She hesitated for a moment, thinking carefully before replying. She knew from our conversations with her, the word needed to be easily remembered in times of stress and high emotion but also a word which would be unlikely to come up in the course of normal conversation or role play. "Yes, m'Lord, i have my safe word. It is *basi*."

basi, in Swahili, means "stop."

"That is acceptable." I nodded. I looked over at Neferterri, who was still on the phone, and she motioned to me that the safe word was acceptable to her as well. "However, you must be aware I will still use My discretion, as your Goddess will, too. If I believe you are using your safe word just to spare yourself from a little punishment, I will not stop right away."

I lifted her face to me to continue my lesson. "Be aware that if you persist in using your safe word at times I deem inappropriate, I will punish you harder and possibly ignore it completely. you must realize that it is to be used ONLY when absolutely necessary."

"Yes, m'Lord, I understand."

"The objective of what we are doing here is to push your boundaries and explore your limits. If you stop before reaching these limits, you will never learn or grow. Do you understand?" I asked.

"Yes, m'Lord, I understand." She heard me move away from her and sit in another chair not far from Neferterri. I could feel her wanting to watch us, but she resisted the temptation, remaining motionless on the floor and awaiting the next command, which soon came from my Beloved.

"Come here." Her voice had an unctuous tone to it. I watched Kitana drop on all fours and crawl toward her, head still bowed. She kneeled before her Goddess, naked and compliant.

"What is Your command of me, my Goddess?"

"I am going to spank you. I want to feel your flesh warming beneath My hand as I punish you while your Sir watches. Assume the position, Kitana."

Kitana complied quickly, the excitement building within her, the anticipation of her Goddess's touch making her shiver. I sat in my chair, watching them, watching the sensuality between women I knew on my best day I could never duplicate.

Something about women together...the heat between them... it was all I could do to keep still; my member starting to awaken.

As Kitana knelt down on all fours between Neferterri's knees, I watched her hand stroke down Kitana's back. Not so much a caress as a voyage of exploration. It continued down across her buttocks, cupping each one in turn before pushing roughly between Kitana's thighs, parting them. Neferterri's fingers encountered the burning wetness of Kitana's labia and I saw Kitana shiver under her touches. They parted Kitana's lips and slid over her clit before Neferterri penetrated two fingers into her silky depths. I heard a moan escape Kitana's lips softly and Neferterri withdrew her fingers immediately. Her voice was still so even, so controlled as she spoke to Kitana.

"This is not for your pleasure, little one, although I can feel from your wetness that you are more than ready for whatever I choose to do next. Let's see how you feel once I begin to punish you."

Kitana let out a loud gasp as Neferterri's palm smacked across her left butt cheek. She had expected the first blow to be lighter, more teasing than punishing, and there she realized her mistake, as I'd hoped she would. This wasn't meant as sexual foreplay as she had previously experienced. This was a lesson in obedience and the weight of the first blow focused her mind. Kitana gasped again as Neferterri slapped her right butt cheek and then bit her bottom lip as she picked up the pace, raining slaps on both cheeks in quick succession. I took quite a delight in watching her caramel-colored flesh begin to redden, and from the way Kitana squirmed between slaps, I imagined her skin was burning and tears welled up in her eyes.

The blows stopped abruptly and Neferterri motioned for me to come over to feel the heat between Kitana's thighs. My hand was mere inches away from her passion, inhaling her scent as if she were my prey more than my conquest. The instant my fingers touched her clit, she came, struggling against the intensity of her orgasm, but unable to hold back. I heard a soft giggle as my fingers played with her clit, teasing it between my fingers as I ignored her constant squirming.

The amusement in my voice was clear, but I kept my composure, stayed in the zone.

After all, she was supposed to learn punishment versus pleasure. "Someone was incredibly turned on considering they were supposed to be being punished. Did I say you could come?" I asked Kitana, my voice booming into her ear.

She fought to find her voice. Her mind was still centered on the sensations my fingers were causing between her thighs, "No, m'Lord, forgive me, i could not control it."

"No!" I shouted as I punctuated the word with another stinging slap to her already pain-soaked cheeks.

"This is another lesson we want you to learn and accept. Control is no longer yours. You will react as we dictate, once you're properly trained. In time, you will be taught to come on command, to bend to our will completely, but it will come in due time; do you understand?"

"Yes, m'Lord." I saw the tears flowing from Kitana's eyes. Even in the position she was in, I could see them falling to the carpet.

"This was a punishment session and we felt you needed to experience true pain to focus you correctly. Now, get to your feet, Kitana." I watched her struggle to her feet, legs weak from orgasm, backside tingly from the sound spanking she'd received from the two of us.

"Understand that even when you are being punished, it is done out of love, baby girl. In order for you to be the best we expect you to be, there will be some bumps and bruises along the way, literally and figuratively," Neferterri instructed. "If we didn't love you, we wouldn't correct you when you mess up."

"Go to the couch and lean over its back. *Now!*" My voice rang out in the otherwise silent room.

Her legs complied almost without conscious thought. She bent over the low back of the couch, ass presented proud and high. We caressed her backside and she flinched as our fingers stroked her burning flesh.

"Nice," I whispered into Kitana's ear. "You should see how red it is. I think, however, it may be necessary to keep your ass covered in the presence of your husband for a while, although I think he will understand considering his Mistress is probably doing the same thing to him."

Without warning, my leather flogger cracked across her ass. The blow, unexpected, forced a scream from Kitana's lips. The biting pain was more intense than anything either of us had inflicted during that session. It caused Kitana to instinctively rise up, but Neferterri's voice stopped her in her tracks.

"Don't you dare stand up or I will double the lashes on top of what Ramesses is doing," she hissed. "You will stay there for another five strokes and I am going to make each one harder. Do you understand?"

"Yes, my Goddess," she whispered as tears began to roll unchecked down her cheeks. The next blow lashed across her ass again, and Kitana's screams rang out in the room louder.

One…

Two…

Three...

Four…

Five…

The pain she inflicted was so intense I thought Kitana was going to faint. The final blow landed and Neferterri moved away from her. She headed into the kitchen as I took control of Kitana from there.

"Stand up and face Me." My breathing was uneven and I knew she could hear the excitement in my voice as she turned and faced me, her face wet with tears. "I want you to kneel and thank us, and I also want you to know we are almost finished here today."

She kneeled slowly before me. The sadist in me roused to the surface, watching her weary body try to maintain its balance. She moved between the space between pain and pleasure, causing me to wake her out of her trance before we lost her to subspace.

My voice boomed in her ear. "Look at Me and thank your Goddess and Me."

I raised her face to mine as she spoke with a trembling voice, "Thank You, m'Lord, my Goddess. Thank You for punishing me as i deserve." Without a further command, her eyes returned to my feet and she knelt quietly awaiting the next command.

At this point, we agreed she'd finally had enough. I went to the couch and picked up a throw blanket. As I unfolded the blanket, Neferterri walked with Kitana over to the couch and carefully sat her down. We wrapped the blanket over her and placed ourselves on each side of her, with Neferterri grabbing some ice chips she'd taken out of the freezer while in the kitchen to help hydrate her slowly.

Kitana was still in tears, and we each took turns drying her face, reassuring her things were okay.

"Shhh, baby, let the ice help you balance. We're still here with you," Neferterri repeated, caressing her face.

After a while, Kitana settled down, her breathing steadying. It was a wonderful way to finish her initiation within the House, and it had us all looking forward to things yet to come.

15 RAMESSES

Every so often you come upon a time in your life when choices can make or break you.

There was a line in one of my favorite movies that went, "*The older your mind gets, the better choices your dick makes.*"

When it came to some of the decisions I made when I was younger, I admit I didn't make the best decisions on the planet, outside of marrying my Beloved. But when it came to the submissives in our lives, the decision was easy. Almost every one of them was over twenty-five, which meant there was no way I was getting caught out there like Master Cypher did over the summer. We had a family to look after, period. Unfortunately, not all of my brethren could hold to those same principles. I mean, who could really blame them? If you, as a man, had a young woman in college who wanted you, especially within the realm of BDSM, how do you say no? I didn't expect someone who I called mentor, who had been like a father to me, to get caught in the same trap.

I was reading a news report online when I heard a loud knock at the door. I raised an eyebrow when I looked through the peephole and saw two police officers standing on my porch.

"May I help you, officers? Is something wrong?" I braced for the impact of what they might have been there for, and really tensed up when I recognized one of the officers as a childhood friend of mine.

"Sorry about this, Sir, but this matter looks pretty serious," the other officer told me as I stood in the doorway. She handed me a document to read over as she explained. "It looks like your friend is gonna be in some severe trouble."

"What? What's the charge?" My eyes moved immediately to my friend, trying to make some sense out of the wording on the documents. I couldn't figure out a lot of the legalities or jargon because I was out of practice, despite my criminology degree, but the two charges stuck out like a sore thumb: *kidnapping and false imprisonment.* My mind was numbing by the minute, trying to understand what was happening, and even more so at the thought of Amenhotep behind bars.

"Could we have a moment, officer? Your partner is a friend of mine," I asked the female officer, who shot me a look before stepping off my porch and heading back to the squad car. I really could have cared less whether she knew or not; she was immaterial. I needed to talk straight with my friend.

"You need to find better partners, D. That one's a little too nosey for my taste," I told Dominic, a long-time friend from our high school days. Had things gone down a different path, we would have been partners on the force together. "So give me the rundown; what is He up against?"

"Don't worry about Niki; she's cool. She has a problem with being dismissed when she's gonna hear about it from me anyway. You know the rap sheet: False imprisonment, simple battery, among other charges, K," Dom flatly answered, which really didn't surprise me. He was doing his job, and his partner didn't know about WIITWD, or "what it is that we do." At least not that I knew about. "There might be some eyes on this one, man. I'm just warning you."

"What eyes are you talking about, D? Shoot me straight here,"

I asked him. I stood toe to toe with him, staring him down. "Who's pissed off? I know you know something, or you wouldn't be this vague."

He knew I was grasping at straws for the most part. I'm not naïve to think Amenhotep didn't have enemies. Hell, I had them, too, but to put a man behind bars started to border into the personal grudge type of situation. I leaned against my front door, rubbing my temples, trying to figure out some method to the madness swirling around in my head.

"Alright, man. I'll do this because we go way back," Dominic confessed, seeing my frustration. "Lieu got at us about the person who filed. Turns out, the person has family that is deeply connected, possibly to the mayor. I can't discuss particulars, but I know you, K; you'll be able to figure this out without much help."

"Who pressed?" I meant, of course, who filed the complaint. I needed to know, not that I was going to do anything about it, but my extended family needed my help.

"You didn't hear this from me, K." He took a breath before he stated safi's real name aloud. He then stepped back and watched me hit the roof in anger.

"Why is it always the young ones? Damn." I threw my hands up in frustration. "Where are you transferring him to?"

"Well, she filed in Fulton, so he's heading up there," he answered, and then informed me, "Once I get him up there, I have to take myself off the case. You already know why."

Yeah, I knew why...he'd been out with us before. Complete conflict of interest.

It's a cop thing. My dad had to do it a few times in his career. It still fucked with me, but I was still a civilian, no matter how much I didn't want to admit it.

But that also meant I could do things he couldn't because of those same limitations. I planned to work those limitations to the hilt.

"Yo, Dom, thanks for the heads-up," I told him as he headed back to the unit. "And tell your partner there are no hard feelings, alright? I'll even throw in some tickets to the Male Revue Neferterri is throwing at the club next week, as a peace offering."

"I'll let her know, K. She might need to release some tension, and I know how wild those things can get." Dominic laughed as he gave me pound. "Oh yeah, make sure he gets a good attorney. She hinted at possible rape charges, too."

16 ∞ RAMESSES

Being in the Fulton County Jail was a bittersweet moment for me.

Before I turned to professional shutterbug, I wanted to be a detective, like my father before me. So, being at the jail wasn't supposed to give me the butterflies in my stomach I felt. It felt like an eternity walking toward the communication area to speak to Amenhotep, but somehow I managed to get there.

Seeing Him on the other side of that window, my heart damn near broke. Here was a man who made me the Dominant I am. Now, here he sat, an accused rapist and kidnapper, eyes completely bloodshot from staying up all night in the holding cell before they moved him to general population. I refused to take pity, though. In my mind He was never guilty in the first place. I was going to move heaven and earth to make sure He came out of this without much of a scratch on him, mainly because I knew He would do the same for me. Family had to look out for each other.

I picked up the receiver, making eye contact with Him for the first time. He looked human to me, after looking like a god for so long. "How are You holding up?"

"Not good, youngster. I'm not even supposed to be in here," Amenhotep stated through the receiver. "Ramesses, I didn't do it. she said awful things, man. Said I raped her…abused her, man."

I sat there and watch helplessly as He was nearly reduced to tears.

The first thing on my mind was whether the other slaves were okay.

"paka came down as soon as she found out. The cops took the computers…everything in the dungeon that wasn't bolted down." Amenhotep repeated what paka had told him earlier. "All of the girls gave statements to dispute what safi told the cops."

"Why the hell would she say such things? You have a reputation within the community. she's got to be aware of that." My anger was boiling and mounting with each passing moment and with each word I spoke.

"Something spooked her. I know it." Amenhotep regained his composure. "Either that, or she's pissed about something. But what was it? I treated her like I treat all My girls."

Yeah, every one of the girls was treated the same way, except for paka. The green-eyed monster was on the loose. Damn.

"I've got some tough questions for You, Sir, and I need straight answers." Ramesses took over inside of me, and it was needed. "How old is safi?"

"*You know better.*" Amenhotep didn't like my tone, but I really didn't care at that point. We were family, yes, but there was no time to look at things with rose-colored glasses. "I taught You, remember that."

"What…was…her…*age?*" I commanded. I didn't back down like I normally did when He asserted Himself and didn't want to answer questions. Too much was at stake.

"Nineteen. Confirmed," Amenhotep replied. "Next."

"What was her status?" I stated, moving on to the next point of fact I needed. By status, I wanted to know in what capacity safi was supposed to serve. In His House there were two categories: sexual and domestic.

"Sexual and domestic." Amenhotep again answered in a monotone voice. "Next."

"Did You corrupt her station?" In asking that question, I meant did she begin to think that she was more than what her station dictated...and more importantly, did He give her the impression she meant more than her station suggested.

"I decline to answer." Amenhotep shut down, pulling His ear away from the receiver.

"Not good enough, Sir," I warned. I motioned for him to place His ear to the receiver. "Rumors will run rampant, and I need ammo to combat things until You post bond."

"How long have we known each other?" Amenhotep asked, pushing His face closer to the glass.

"Sir, You are My mentor, and I love You like a father, but I need and I *will* get full disclosure." I was blunt about my intentions, even if the answer would hurt.

"*Yes, I did!*" Amenhotep stared me straight in the eyes, suddenly convinced of His own innocence. "I did nothing wrong, Ramesses. You, above all others, should know that."

"*Have You lost your mind?!?!?!?!* You may have violated Your core rules, Sir," I scolded. "This will make things extremely messy."

"her state of mind was solid, Ramesses," Amenhotep said, getting more demonstrative by the minute. "she belongs to Me, in any manner I see fit. Who are *You* to judge Me, Sir?"

"What did she do to You for You to act this way?" I asked Him again, getting as close to the glass as he was. This was a showdown, whether we liked it or not. Time to throw down, and whoever backed down first, lost. I saw the fire in His eyes, looking at me like I was some cut-rate novice challenging His kingdom.

"You would never understand, and You never will! she..." And all of a sudden, He simply shut down. "None of the other girls betrayed Me the way she did. So, I dismissed her from the House."

This look of pure shock raced through me as I heard those words.

In the fifteen years I had known Amenhotep, He had *never* dismissed a collared slave from His House. That was not to say that there hadn't been a few who no longer wanted favor from Him or wanted release from service, but once the collar was placed, something severe would have to go down to have the collar removed.

"she tried to meet with another Dominant. she even called Me to lie about being at work late," Amenhotep began. "What she failed to realize was that once she fucked him, he called Me to try and humiliate Me. Rubbing it in My face, saying I was washed up as a Dominant if He could take one from Me."

Things were becoming clearer, but they were about to get messier.

"After I punished her, I don't know what came over Me, but I used her like a Midtown whore. In My mind, she was damaged goods, and no longer deserved to be in My House." He finally finished His account.

He had done it. He broke one of His core rules a Dominant swears to: He must be in control of Himself at *all* times, to do no harm. In that split-second that night, Amenhotep had reduced Himself from a regally respected Dominant to nothing more than a jealous pimp on the street.

paka and two of the service slaves arrived, paka tapping my shoulder to alert me of their presence behind me. I gave paka the receiver and stood close by in case He needed to speak to me again. The smile on His face as they spoke let me know this part of the nightmare was soon to be over. The other two girls found an open table to sit as they awaited paka and the conclusion of the conversation.

"We've posted bond for You, my Master. You may leave with us as soon as possible," paka stated as she spoke through the receiver to Him.

I saw the connection between the two of them, and another piece of this puzzle became clearer. Whether He wanted to admit it or not, Amenhotep and paka had fallen for each other.

I left them to their conversation, as I didn't feel it was my place to intervene or eavesdrop on the exchange. After all, there are things between a Dominant and submissive that were not for public consumption. I sat with the other slave girls to keep the leering inmates who were in the area from making them too uncomfortable. It was the least I could do to keep my urges at bay to find out what the conversation was about.

Still, despite all of the years paka served at her Master's feet, this could have been the only logical conclusion, the culmination of all of those years of being with Him.

I wasn't blind, but I guess I chose not to see.

At the end of the day, I guess I should have seen this coming a mile away.

17 ⚭ RAMESSES

As I had suspected, the mailing lists were abound with news of Amenhotep's arrest.

Some were upset about it; others were venomous in their criticism of what He had supposedly done to "poor" safi—not to mention the haters that got on their soapbox about how "this would never have happened if she were a black submissive" bullshit. Sooner or later, the race card would be put out there.

I was in a quandary of sorts. What the hell should I do, knowing what I knew? My mentor was in the wrong, even though the situation did call for dismissal, according to protocol. With safi gone into hiding, so to speak, it would make finding the truth much more difficult.

Neferterri got home with the kids and was surprised to see enough IM windows to cause stimulation overload.

"What the hell happened this time?" she asked as the kids headed toward the family room to watch TV. "I expected turnout for Amenhotep's Halloween party, but damn."

Before I could get the words out of my mouth, our oldest ran into the kitchen to where I was working, shouting, "Uncle Amen's on the TV!"

My worst fears had been realized. We rushed to turn on the TV in the kitchen in time to see the cameras showing Amenhotep, paka, and the other two girls leave in the SUV.

"Honey, go in the other room and watch a movie with your sisters, okay? Mommy's got to get some answers," she told our daughter.

Once they skipped out of sight, Neferterri turned to me with a confused look on her face. "Okay, what was that about?"

As I broke the whole story down to her, detail by detail, I saw my wife's face turn to stone before my eyes.

"He's going to get crucified in the media for this," she stated. "No one will touch Him for fear of getting burned themselves, baby."

"I know, baby. The only way to get this out of the way is to find safi and hopefully get her to drop the charges," I stressed. One thing I knew for sure, where there's smoke, there's fire. As long as the vanilla world didn't know about it, the community as a whole could continue to function without the microscope.

Neferterri closed her eyes before she quietly uttered, "Do what You have to do, just as long as it doesn't affect our family or our House. This is important. If the information in Amenhotep's computers comes out..."

She didn't have to say anything more to get her point across. A lot of people would be exposed, including us, and a lot were nowhere near ready to be brought out into the light. This was going to take a lot of finesse, not to mention built-up goodwill and some luck to get this done.

But first things first...I needed to find safi.

18 ⊗ RAMESSES

See…this was why I didn't want to be a cop in the first place.

I went through every low-lying, sneaky, down-right ugly source at my disposal to get a location on safi.

When all of this drama went down, she literally tried to drop off the map, but fortunately she was sloppy in her disappearance. I began to pick up the clues that eventually led me to her.

It took me a few days, but my digging eventually turned up gold. It turned out safi was the daughter of a well-to-do businessman up in Dalton, north of the Atlanta area, and word began to get back to him concerning the activities of his little girl. That wasn't what set him off, since he was also a swinger up in that area. What got him going was that she had become a part of a "harem," as he was told, and of course he couldn't have his daughter be a part of such a thing. Put two and two together, add the call to the mayor, and there's the instant newsworthy story.

The next bread crumb came in the form of safi's former roommate, emphasis on the "former." She was more than happy to help out since safi's father had cut off the money flow, and safi ended up leaving her high and dry with a condo she could barely afford.

What was it they say about burning bridges?

This child was about to end up on an island with no one to turn to for help. The information the roommate gave me eventually led me to an unexpected source: the Dom safi was messing around with.

Now, this guy turned out to be what I like to call an M.I.D., or "Master of Internet Domination." The ones who have no references to speak of and no one to vet for them, but they are a Dominant in their own mind. These dudes usually are married to a vanilla woman who "would never understand" WIITWD, so they hide it from them and live this other life as an honorable Dominant.

What a joke, and the funny part was, he fit the profile to the letter.

Upon further inspection of this "Dom" through some of my connections to the Dominants that knew of him—some who were and some who were not too fond of him—I found out he held a grudge against Amenhotep because he did not prove himself true to the teachings of his Mentor, who happened to be very good friends with Amenhotep.

Like Amenhotep wasn't going to check him out first?

Going a little deeper, and "Master" Judah, as he called himself, runs one of safi's father's businesses, an auto body repair shop in Dalton. Now, I'd bet you a night's worth of table dances at Liquid as to who I think dropped a dime on Amenhotep?

I figured out the best way to handle things without getting too caught up was to catch ol' boy at his job. It's easier to be civilized when your job's on the line. Besides, if I played my cards right, I had a trump card that would get me the information I needed without getting hostile. So, I called in a favor from a friend within the swinger community who takes pictures at parties. The information he provided me and the pictures to prove it were jaw-dropping, to say the least!

I only hoped to play this information to my best ability. A lot of lives depended on it.

☥

He saw me coming in the door of the shop and approached me like I was some lost tourist who had no business in his shop. He tried to sound congenial, but I felt the suspicion in his voice. "Hi, sir, how may we help you today?"

"Yes, I have business with Mr. Ronin, safi's father," I replied, using her submissive name to get his attention. I didn't have time to mince words with this dude, especially when he regarded me as inferior the moment I stepped into his world.

Judah's face turned red for a moment, and then he replied, "You're not getting your friend off, bro. He fucked with the wrong girl."

"Is that a fact?" I kept my cool as I said it. I was in enemy territory without backup, and I needed to be smart. "Well, maybe you might have the exact same problem yourself, huh? You know, someone fucking the wrong girl?"

I massaged my chin to let the message sink in.

When Judah heard that comment, he froze up. "Wha…what do you mean?"

"Well, let's see, I had a P.I. friend of mine do a check of the phone number safi used to have her new 'Dom' call my friend to inform him of what His safi was doing," I said, starting my smokescreen. "Unfortunately, he couldn't get a trace on the number."

I saw Judah relax, figuring he hadn't been busted. But once I pulled out the manila envelope, his eyes got wide. "What's in the envelope, man?"

"Well, while he wasn't able to get an exact trace on the number, he was, however, able to triangulate the location of where the call came from, which led me to you. He also managed to get me something that I think you might be interested in seeing disappear. So, consider this your version of *Let's Make a Deal:* you give me safi's location, and I don't send this to your wife and boss. By the way, when's the baby due?" I tapped the envelope to prove I was serious. "I'm sure Mr. Ronin wouldn't want to see the contents of this folder, now, would he?"

"You'd destroy me over some pussy, man?" Judah tried to call my bluff. "You ain't got the balls, man. Besides, he won't believe someone like you over me."

"Well, I guess when you get home tonight, you'll find out, huh?" I wasn't too thrilled at the "someone like you" comment, but I had to remember I was in North Georgia as well. I turned around to walk out. "Take care."

"*No!*" Judah reactively grabbed my arm to stop me. I looked at him like he was two steps shy of catching a beat down if he didn't let my arm go. He finally relented. "Okay, dude, you win. She's at her girlfriend's house. I'll get You the address."

He headed over to write the information down, still shaking as he wrote.

And he's a Dominant? I kept saying to myself.

"Alright, a deal's a deal. Give me the envelope," Judah angrily demanded.

"For someone in your position, you sure are hostile," I joked, even though he didn't find it all that funny. It was wild to see him squirm though. It almost made me forget about that dumb-ass comment he made toward me earlier. "I thought the customer was always right?"

I took a lighter and set the envelope on fire. As it slowly began to burn, I told him, "Now, I'm going to assume you're a man of good faith, in that you gave me what I wanted. But if I find out it is bogus information..."

"I gave you what you wanted, dude. My wife will miscarry if she gets any stressful news." Judah pleaded with me, his eyes fixated on the burning envelope.

"Okay. I guess I can believe you, since you put it that way." I dropped the envelope in the trash can outside so that it would burn itself out. "As far as I am concerned, your wife knows nothing about your late nights working overtime, right?"

"Alright, damn." Judah slumped in a chair, looking like he had been through a couple of rounds of boxing. "Just leave. I have customers to attend to. You being here is bad for business."

"Perhaps I should stick around, just to see how bad I am for business." I looked at a couple of women who were quite enamored with seeing a six-foot-seven black man looking like he stepped out of *GQ* magazine. "Ladies, do you think I'm bad for an establishment such as this?"

The ladies started to giggle, which really upset Judah. But I knew he couldn't say anything derogatory or else those same ladies might've told their husbands the manager was a prick.

So much for "bad business," I guess.

Heading back to my car, I glanced at the Marietta address on the slip of paper, realizing I had been to that house before. I kinda felt bad for ol' boy though. I mean he never took the time to see the pictures of his wife...his *pregnant* wife...having sex with, of all people, Mr. Ronin himself. Oh well, so much for her being fragile, especially considering the flexible positions she was able to do in those photos.

No wonder his job was safe.

19 ⊗ RAMESSES

"How did you find me???"

safi panicked when she came home to find me sitting on her front porch, chatting with her friend, chastity. Then, she smirked. "i should have You arrested for stalking me. i left Your precious Mentor, and He got what He deserved for treating me like a whore."

Now, in my younger days, I probably would have strung that little girl up by her ankles and whipped her within an inch of her life for the lies that she's told. Her body language alone let me know that she didn't tell the whole truth to the police about what happened that night. My guess was that she had to lie to keep herself out of the fire. But that didn't matter. I needed to keep my calm in order for this plan to work. If I didn't, she could've easily charged me with assault, even with chastity there as a witness.

"Well, I actually didn't find you, love. you see, chastity is a collared submissive of My friend, Master Altar, or had you forgotten that?" I sort of lied, but she didn't need to know the truth about her new "Dom" dropping a dime on her to save his own skin. "I gave Him a call and told Him I was in the area, and He wanted Me to stop by and check on His property for Him. Running into you was an unexpected bonus."

I tried to warn her the community was very small.

"Whatever he told You, he's lying," safi lashed out. I had a feeling

Judah might have punked out and warned her I was in the area, but she would have never come home if he had tipped her off to my whereabouts.

"Sorry, girl, but you knew better than to file a false report," chastity scolded her. "It's not my fault that your dad found out and threatened to disown you. your lies have caught up with you."

"you did what?!?!?!" I couldn't keep my composure any longer. My suspicions were confirmed, and I was ready to rip her to shreds.

"What was i supposed to do? you know how my daddy is!" safi turned on the water works quickly, but the tears didn't work on either one of us. She was more worried about losing daddy's money than putting an innocent man behind bars.

"So, what happens when the rape kit comes back and it shows you had sex with more than one man that night?" chastity asked, getting angrier by the minute. "See, it's bitches like you that fuck things up for the rest of us, you fake-ass wannabe. It's hard enough being a good submissive, especially for my Master, but word's gonna get out about your lie, and my reputation and my Master's reputation will be damaged just for you being here against His wishes!"

"My dad's going to kill me if he finds out the truth!" safi yelled. "i don't give a damn about this bullshit community! i'm sorry i even got myself into this mess!"

"safi, look, if I gave you something I believe will smooth things over and have your old man chill out about this whole mess, will you drop the charges against Amenhotep?" I had to put a stop to this hysteria, or things would spiral out of control. I didn't have time for little girls overreacting because their small insignificant world would be shattered if the truth came out. Besides, we have enough problems in the community without weekend players trying to be real about something they don't understand, and don't care to understand as long as they get their pleasure out of it.

safi nodded, and I went back to the car to get the other copy of the pictures I'd used to squeeze Judah.

Yeah, I know, I can be a cold-hearted bastard sometimes. But when it comes to the protection of my family, and my House, I will do whatever it takes…even if it meant destroying a man's image in the eyes of his daughter in the process.

safi's face turned beet red, but she understood this was the leverage she needed to keep her old man's mouth shut, and hell, maybe even get more money out of him from then on out. It was then she realized maybe "this bullshit community" could offer her more than the vanilla friends she thought were so much better than us.

safi lowered her eyes and bowed in respect. "my Lord, i am in Your debt. i will do as You request," she stated quietly, looking at the envelope. "Please forgive me for the way i spoke earlier. But i think that i might have damaged myself for another Dominant to find me worthy. i mean, Judah wasn't even worth the trouble. What am i going to do now?"

"Things should work out fine, safi, and don't worry about the rumors. They eventually go away," I reassured her as I got in my car to leave. "you may use Me to vet for you once you've completed your task for Me. you have My word."

I was mentally exhausted by the time I got home.

I guess this was what my father felt like when he came home from tough cases. I guess in some ways, his career as a detective did rub off on me. I didn't have it in me to be a police detective, no matter how much it was "in my blood."

I got through the door and my senses kicked in quickly, noticing the house was quieter than usual.

"Mercedes?" I called upstairs.

No answer.

That didn't sit well with me. Usually she texted me to let me know if she was leaving the house.

I assumed the kids weren't home; otherwise one of them would have said something as soon as the door opened. So, I slowly headed my way upstairs to draw a bath and soak for a little while, deducing Neferterri was at her mom's with the kids. That was fine. I needed some time to myself to get the day's events out of my system.

Imagine my surprise in seeing Kitana and shamise in our bedroom, completely naked—one with soap in her hand, the other with a towel and baby oil in hers, both on their knees waiting on me. While under normal circumstances it would be a wondrous sight to behold, it left me in a state of confusion. I quickly got over it and found some energy within me to conjure up my Dominant persona.

"I'm too exhausted to argue as to why the two of you are here," I said, still standing in the doorway with my mouth hanging open.

"Goddess summoned us here, m'Lord. She said we had an important task to complete once You got home," Kitana stated.

"It's time to take care of You tonight, Daddy," shamise sweetly cooed as she normally did when she looked forward to pampering me. "Sometimes it is okay to let go and release energy. Isn't that what You taught us?"

As much as I hated to admit it, shamise was right. Tonight was not about me giving up control. This was about releasing the negative energy I had acquired while trying to clear Amenhotep. So, rather than resist my girls, I simply undressed, headed toward the hot bath awaiting me, and released.

20 ⚭ RAMESSES

After playing P.I. all weekend, I decided to take some time to myself and try to get my wind back.

I got my apprentice to run the studio for a couple of days while I took a mini-vacation. Nothing to get out of town, mind you, but I needed to get my batteries recharged.

I surprised the kids by making breakfast before they headed off to school, which kept Neferterri in bed for a change. That didn't last long once she found herself getting raped almost as soon as the bus picked the kids up. Outside of parties and such, this was one of those rare times where I got to treat my wife like a wanton slut, and she could scream her head off without fear of waking the kids at night.

Once she headed off to work with an afterglow and a big smile on her face, I parked myself on the couch to watch nothing but football, football, FOOTBALL.

At least, that was the plan anyway. But you know what they say about the best-laid plans, of course?

The phone rang, and the caller ID let me know it was coming from Jay's home. *What the hell was this about?* I asked myself as I picked up the phone. "Hello?"

"Yo, Kane, it's me, dawg. Sorry about calling from the house." Jay sounded a little off, like he had done something stupid and was afraid to admit it.

"Why are you at your soon-to-be ex-wife's house? I thought you were done with her?" I had to ask the question because I knew Jasmine's off days were usually on a Monday, and at the time he was calling, he was supposed to be at work.

"Man, I don't know. I was trying to pick up some stuff from the house to put in storage, and she came downstairs. Before I could say anything, she started kissing me," Jay started.

"Come on, Jay? You're gonna complicate things, man." I tried to convince my boy, until he dropped a bomb on me.

"Naw, Kane, I'm saying…when I tried to back her off, I felt another pair of hands on me. I turned around, and it was Selena, my secretary," Jay explained. "Before I knew it, she said, 'I'll let you keep her if you come back to me and we can work things out.' I caved, but what else could I do, dawg? She got me twisted, especially when I was trying to have Selena anyway."

He had a point, and I knew it. Damn, Jasmine pulled out all the stops, bringing his secretary into the mix. What man would have said no in that situation? Anger goes out the window in a scenario like that. Who was I to tell him what he needed to do with his marriage? But I already knew what he was getting himself into.

The question was, did he know?

"Looks like Jasmine might have realized what she might have been losing after all?" I queried. "If she's serious about her offer, I'd say go for it, but approach with extreme caution."

"Yeah, but she still hurt me, dawg. How the hell do I get past that?" he asked me. "Last night was wonderful, but it was just one night."

"It's like I told you before, man, you have to figure out what's best for you. I can't do it for you, no one can." I thought back to Jasmine's threats from a month ago, and I couldn't help but wonder why she did a 180 so quickly.

But in truth, I didn't know Jasmine well enough to know any better about anything. I didn't want to believe she would have anything to do with that car spying on the house a few weeks back. I made myself a mental note to check with my father's connections at the Department of Motor Vehicles to find out who owned the car.

Jay changed the subject on me before I dwelled on things too much. "Yo, I heard you got ol' girl to drop the charges on Amenhotep. I don't know how you pulled off that trick, but remind me to invest some major loot into your P.I. firm when you get the chance."

"Hell no, man." I almost spit out my soda. "You know that's not me."

"Yeah, whatever, Shaft," he managed to say while laughing. "Look, gotta head into the job for a while, are we still on for *Monday Night Football* at the bar?"

"Yeah, I'm down. Holla." I hung up the phone and went back to my football highlights from the weekend without a further thought about the conversation.

☥

While some guys go to a normal sports bar for *Monday Night Football*, me and the boys go to Magic City in downtown Atlanta.

I mean, come on? You can watch football and get a lap dance at the same time. Yeah, I know, I could always go to Liquid, but it's too much like going to work.

We stepped in the club after dropping money for the cover, and Ice had already spotted one of the dancers he normally spent money on, so we sat in the area she worked to get our ball on.

"Yo, J, what's up with you and Jazzy? I thought the final hearing was in a few weeks?" Ice asked while slipping a ten-spot in baby girl's G-string.

"Man, last night was about getting mine. I mean, my wife is fine, dammit," Jay replied.

"Yeah, but so is Candy, and she ain't got no baggage," Ice countered. "From what Kane told me, she was pissed you split when she was more than ready to give you sum."

"Naw, I'm still tripping off you being somebody's boy toy and submissive, dawg. What's up with that?" Jay took offense that Ice was dismissing Jasmine so quickly, which didn't make any sense to me. They were getting divorced, after all. "Thought you were supposed to be top dawg?"

Ice stopped dead in his tracks.

I saw his eyes grow small, and I knew Jay had gotten personal. Even the dancer in his lap knew she needed to be somewhere else at that exact moment. Much like when birds fly away in droves at the first sign of danger, it didn't take a rocket scientist to realize the conversation was about to go downhill quickly.

"You can ignore the fact that you're slipping all you want, Jay. The fact remains is you're getting weak." Then, Ice pulled the snap of the night. "Better to be a willing participant and get a nut out of it than to be forced to wear your wife's panties and suffer in shame."

It was obvious from Jay's demeanor there was some information kept from me, and I could understand why. I saw Jay's face, and his manhood, hit the floor, which lent credence to Ice's claims. Jay turned pale, which was hard for a dark-skinned brother to do, and I didn't know whether to laugh or cry. There was no way in hell I would have let some information slip out like that, even on my most vulnerable and drunken night.

"Naw, man, are you serious?!?!?!" I asked, but it was too late. Jay got up out of his seat and walked away without another word. I sat there for a minute, confused at what went down. Meanwhile, Ice had summoned his favorite back over to finish her lap dances.

"Yo, K let him go, man. He needs to get his mind right before he comes back to the game." Ice was still fixated on baby girl, not throwing another care in Jay's direction after he sliced and diced him down to next to nothing. "He asked for it; you saw it yourself."

I figured it was better to try and find Jay to see if his head was screwed on right before assuming too much, so I got up to see where he'd drifted to. Besides, game time wouldn't be for about thirty minutes anyway, so I could play Dr. Phil in enough time to get back to the fun we were supposed to be having.

"Alright, man, talk to me." I finally found him at the bar with a few empty shot glasses already in front of him.

"Your boy needs to keep his fucking mouth shut," Jay blasted. "I got enough issues without his happy-go-lucky ass trying to pour salt in the wounds."

"Man, your ego's bruised, no harm, no foul," I told him, slapping the back of his shoulder. I still had to shake the image Ice had painted out of my head though. Damn. "So, what's the deal; you staying with Jasmine or what?"

"That's the problem, K. I don't know." He threw back another shot. "I know she's not it anymore. But last night...I hadn't had any in a few weeks, so, she caught me slipping."

"What do you mean a few weeks?" Now that was an eye-opener. I knew he and Candy were trying to hold off until the divorce, but I was still confused. "What about Kitana? I thought that she..."

"I told her to lie to you," Jay confessed, putting his head in his hands. "She started on me, and I couldn't do it...my body was willing, but she knew. Jazzy's got my mind, and I can't let go. Even Candy's at the end of her rope with me."

I had heard about this type of thing happening to men when they were getting divorced. They get so caught up in the marriage and the wife, that when it's time to get out there and date again, they freeze up, going back to what's safe at home. It made me thankful, and humbled, I had the woman in my life in Neferterri, and being happily married.

Rather than beat him up even more, I gave him a fair warning. "You're gonna have to man up, sooner rather than later. Women pick up on weakness, whether they are in the lifestyle or not."

"I know, dawg. I need to stay away from my wife until the court proceedings are over," Jay concluded.

"Good. Now can we get back to the game?" I asked, pointing in Ice's direction. "Maybe see some ass shaking in the process?"

We got up from the bar and headed back to our area, when someone grabbed Jay from behind and spun him around. I tried to get a gauge on the situation quick, before Jay's temper got the best of him.

"I'm hoping you think you know me to be grabbing me like that, bruh." Jay was already on dude before I could grab him. In the corner of my eye, I could see Ice picking up and heading in our direction.

"Naw, homey, but we do have your bitch of a wife in common though," he said. This guy was hostile. I could feel the heat on him. "Your bitch gave me and my boy the clap the night you caught us with her."

"You're a liar!" Jay countered. Suddenly the deeper wounds from that night came rising furiously to the surface all over again. *"I should have taken care of you both that night!"*

"I'd suggest you check your bitch and make sure, partner," he warned before walking away. He shoved a dancer out of his way as he stormed out the main entrance of the club.

I had to hold on to Jay to keep him from continuing after him, and Ice made sure to provide backup in case he slid from my grip.

But the damage had already been done. There was some severe trouble on the horizon, and if that guy was right, a lot of people could be affected.

"What was that about, Jay?" Ice asked.

"I don't know, but he just helped me make a decision." Jay gritted his teeth, the anger still consuming him. "Jasmine's done. I don't want to see that bitch again."

21 ∞ RAMESSES

It had been a couple of weeks since the incident at Magic City.

I was still reeling from the venom the dude had spat when he'd seen Jay at the club. If what he'd said was true, then Jasmine may have cheated on him with some other people as well. This was getting really thick, really quick. To make sure, I advised my boy to go get tested to make sure he was clear. Luckily, the tests came back negative on everything, including HIV.

October was rolling around the corner fast, which meant that Amenhotep's Halloween party was coming up. Whatever problems Jay had to work out, he was on his own for a while. I couldn't be all to everyone, especially when I had my own House to deal with, both in and out of the alternative world.

There's a term my father always used: "addition by subtraction." Being a photographer, I employed that strategy all the time because people do cancel, sometimes at the last minute. It served me well in my alternative life as well, because submissives can leave you as quickly, sometimes through the fault of no one at all.

I wasn't prepared for the gauntlet that unexpectedly got thrown down in front of me, though.

jamii called me completely out of the blue to let me know she wanted to be released from service. She didn't know whether to be pissed or scared of my calmness to her request. But frankly speaking, why get upset? Almost all of the time, submissives leave for two reasons: they're not happy and they've found another Dominant they thought would treat them better than you, or they want to return to a vanilla lifestyle because things didn't go exactly as planned when they entered this lifestyle. I've always likened the latter to wanting to go back to "prison," but that's my opinion.

In the end, she sounded almost hurt I didn't put up more of a fight. The truth was I saw it coming, ever since the safi's collaring, when she kept silently begging for my attention the entire night. Within a Poly House of multiple submissives, a submissive had to have a certain mentality to handle the fact that the primary focus would not be on them all of the time. Each of the girls knew it before presenting themselves as willing submissives within the House.

But that's what happens when you start reading those BDSM romance novels. That's not reality, and I don't know anyone who has lived that life. I mean, come on? A twenty-something or thirty-something male knowing all there is to know about domination and submission without stepping one foot into the real-time community to learn what it took a lot of us decades to perfect?

If you believed that, I have a lovely home in Agra, India I would love to sell to you.

She called herself trying to disrespect by sending her collar back to us via mailing, but what she did was anger Neferterri, who promptly found out who the new Dominant was she had turned to for "more personal attention" and informed him of the disrespect of her act. He, in a rare act of respect for us, immediately discontinued his consideration of her as his submissive.

As quiet as it was kept, respect and honor were a part of the way things were done around there. So, as a thank you for his display of respect, Amenhotep released one of His service slaves interested in acquisition into the gentleman's service. jamii ended up moving out of Atlanta altogether after that.

I guess she thought she could pick up and find what she wanted somewhere else.

The last thing I remembered hearing about jamii, she had decided to leave the lifestyle and find a vanilla boyfriend because the lifestyle had "bored" her. She can front all she wanted, but the bottom line was she tried to act like the victim and got burned by her own BS. In the process of trying to exact whatever revenge she thought she was going to get, she completely screwed herself out of a good opportunity. As I said before, this was a realm of honor and respect, and what was given, was also received.

nuru was the next to go, and it happened less than a week later.

She started to purposely break the rules in an attempt to get attention as well. That really did nothing more than to upset us. In my pursuit of Angel and Kitana, I guess it was supposedly my fault neither I nor Neferterri paid attention to her. Or should I say *enough* attention to her. Here we go with those damn romance books again. But instead of trying to release her without backlash, we simply punished her with the silent treatment. The one thing we couldn't tolerate was a disobedient submissive for the sake of being disobedient. She was also forbidden from keeping in touch with either Kitana or shamise.

After a week, she simply faded to black, literally. We checked at her apartment to make sure she was in one piece, but we were greeted by an eviction notice on her door. Word got around after nuru disappeared; she had been placed behind bars due to a warrant that she had in her hometown.

Damn.

When I checked on the warrant, it turned out she had been busted on narcotics offenses from an old boyfriend who had dropped a dime on her before she'd come to Atlanta. Oh well, I guess you never really know a person, even after a year of service.

But the one that really hurt was shamise asking for her release, after being with us the longest. Her vanilla boyfriend asked her to marry him, and he had taken a more lucrative position with a company on the West Coast. Although she didn't want to be released, common sense had to take over because we were not big fans of long distance relationships, D/s or otherwise. Even in the Internet age, it's not practical.

"i don't want to leave, Daddy."

"This isn't pleasant for Me either, baby girl. But you made it clear, you want to be with this man, and he's moving across the country for his new position."

"i know. i know You would never want me to choose between him and You and my Goddess, but i can't leave this House. Is there another way?"

"There is, but it would require you to choose between your D/s family or your vanilla life. I can make that choice for you, but I don't know how well you would like that choice."

I heard shamise softly tearing up over the phone. I understood where she was coming from, I truly did. This was something that was dealt with a lot—the balance between keeping a vanilla profile and enjoying being a libertine and a kinkster.

She was the last one I wanted to take a hard line with, but I didn't have a choice.

"Daddy, i don't want to be released, but i want to be with him, too."

"The only way that this will work is if he stays here in Atlanta. If he's insistent upon leaving for L.A. and you choose to leave with him, then we have to release you."

I heard the angst in her voice, and it tore me up she felt this way.

"i'm sorry You feel that way, Daddy. i wish to be released."

"I can hear it in your voice, shamise, you don't want to be released. Why are you torturing yourself and us like this?"

I didn't want to let her go, but she knew the protocols of the House. She's our Alpha submissive, not someone who could be easily replaced, and I didn't want to replace her. Not even Kitana would be able to completely do that. In time, maybe, but that void would be a hard one to fill for the foreseeable future.

As much as I didn't want to admit it, it was perfectly obvious: we loved her without question. I wasn't about to give in without a fight.

"He loves me, Daddy."

"We love you, shamise. you belong to us; you know this is true."

"Tell me what to do, Daddy, *please.*"

This was starting to roll downhill quicker than I wanted, and I felt my grasp slipping by the minute. By the time Neferterri came through the door and saw the expression on my face, she knew something had to be done or else a bond, once so strong, would never be remade.

I quickly explained the situation before giving her the phone. I needed a break to gather my thoughts.

"Baby girl, this is Neferterri. Daddy explained to Me what's going on." Neferterri went into negotiation mode, something I was unwilling to do. "Do you really love this man?"

"Yes, Goddess, that's why this is killing me."

"I know, baby, I can see it on your Daddy's face. Is there any way that we can find a happy compromise?" she asked.

"Goddess, if You both would consider letting me travel to You, at Your whim, i will handle the rest of the details with my soon-to-be husband."

"We can't ask you to do that, shamise. It would put you in a difficult position, one we would not be comfortable asking you to do."

"But i don't want to lose You." Her emotions were on the brink of meltdown, the same as where she was with me.

"Okay, let's slow this down a bit." Neferterri rubbed her temples as she tried to think a minute. "shamise, what we will do is this: we will temporarily release you while you make your transition to L.A. What I mean is for a few months, you will not be obligated to this House in any way, until things start to settle down in your vanilla life out there with your fiancé. After those few months pass, which will put us into the New Year, We will send for you, so we all can assess where things stand and move from there. Do you understand Me, baby girl?"

"Yes, Goddess, that sounds agreeable. Will i be allowed to keep my name?"

"No, baby girl, your name belongs within this House. Protocol obligates us to take your name back, for now. But it will never be given to another submissive within our charge; do you understand Me?"

"Yes, Goddess, i understand. If things progress as we all would hope, will i be given the opportunity to earn my name back, or be given a new one more proper to the House?"

"Yes, baby girl. Right now, you need to follow the path you have chosen. We will always be here. Just because you don't have your physical collar does not mean that you won't be able to feel the eyes of Kemet-Ka on you."

As much as I didn't want to sound callous, knowing Neferterri and I had Kitana and Angel waiting in the wings took the sting of losing shamise away a little bit. Still, as a Dominant, you really never wanted to lose any of your submissives, mainly because separation anxiety took effect. After all, you shared a lot with that person, and some of it was very intense, very intimate. At the same time, life moved on. I was not willing to go through the anxiety with shamise—not after three years of blissful servitude.

I kissed my Beloved. She could tell I was emotionally exhausted from the whole ordeal, as was she. But hearing our little one breathe a sigh of relief with the contingency plan laid out for her to follow was better than losing her altogether. Perhaps a long distance D/s union could be fashioned? Who knew what the future held?

"You know she'll be home again soon, Beloved, right?" Neferterri wiped the tears from my eyes as she sat in my lap. I wiped the tears from hers as we shared a kiss to console each other.

"I know, Beloved," I answered. I wasn't completely convinced of my response to her question, but I wanted to believe in my heart she would be. "It still hurts to have her away from us."

"We'll be fine, darling," she said. "Things have a way of working themselves out; we simply have to be patient."

22 ⊗ RAMESSES

Solitude…that was what I needed.

It was my way of protecting myself against the depression of losing shamise. The best way I could accomplish that was to dive into work for a few days until those feelings dissipated. The only problem was there was no way to know how long I would need to do that. It had been years since something like this had happened, and that was before I married Neferterri.

It was still worth a shot.

I was on the phone with a client in my studio a few hours later to try and take my mind off of the situation I found myself in.

I needed to clear my head and focus a little bit, and I knew I could do that at the studio, especially considering I had a few projects I needed to complete before the deadlines snuck up on me. Technically we still had shamise but had to refer to her by the vanilla nickname she had before we claimed her: Scarlett. After three years of loving servitude within the House, it felt strange to refer to her as Scarlett again. I kept convincing myself that it was only temporary, that she would be back within the House by year's end.

I was negotiating a weekend shoot with my client when Amenhotep and paka stepped through the door. He seemed a bit more content than usual, and paka did, too, now that I thought about it. I simply smiled as I finished the call with my client and let them browse around the studio.

Once I was off the phone, I walked to them both, embracing Amenhotep and giving paka a kiss on the cheek.

"So, what do I owe the honor of this visit?" I asked. "I usually don't see You out this early in the afternoon, Sir."

He looked at me with the same seriousness He had when a glass separated the space between us, when He was on the wrong side of prison bars. Soon, His lips spread into a smile, and He said in His best imitation of Don Corleone from *The Godfather*, "Ramesses, I'm gonna make You an offer You cannot refuse."

"What the hell are You talking about, Amenhotep?" It was hard to place where the calmness was coming from, but I knew Him well enough to know that something was up and whatever it was, it was big.

"I'm leaving, kid," He flatly stated, His mind made up. "It's time."

After dealing with the losses within my House, I didn't think I was quite prepared for His announcement. "Do You mind running that by Me again?"

"I'm leaving Atlanta. There's nothing left to accomplish here, My old friend," Amenhotep stated, His eyes smiling as He said it. "It's time for the next phase of My evolution to begin, as well as Yours, youngster."

This was starting to be a bit more than I bargained for today.

Sure, I was getting over losing my girls, but to lose my mentor and trusted friend might have been the straw to break the camel's back. After all, He was close to our family, our kids. A lot of people within the local community would be greatly affected by His departure.

I broke down for the first time in a long time, like I was preparing for a death in the family.

But this was not a death.

Amenhotep was simply moving on, after fifteen years in Atlanta.

He could see the distress in my eyes, trying to get a grip on the situation. "Do not get upset, Ramesses. This is a time to celebrate, for Me and for You. There will be a great many changes occurring at the beginning of the year."

Celebrate? For me? Confusion swept over my body like a tidal wave. The last thing I wanted to do was celebrate anything. I looked at paka, and she noticed my anxiety as well, and she silently looked to her Master for permission to offer comfort. Once permission was granted, she guided me to a chair and began to gently and expertly rub my shoulders.

As she rubbed my worry away, Amenhotep continued. "There are some things that I will need for You to sign off on, Ramesses. Some things You will be taking ownership of. Others, You will be helping Me control from here."

My mind began to clear, thanks to paka, and I realized I needed all my faculties to grasp exactly what He might be turning over to me. "Taking ownership of what, exactly?"

His smile confirmed what I suspected. "You will be taking over the Palace for starters, Ramesses."

paka, with permission from her Master, added, "Including a few of the service slaves in the house, m'Lord. They have been informed of my Master's departure, and the first question they had concerned You and whether You would be taking over ownership of the house and the slaves within."

My head was killing me, to say the least. But it was about to be sent into more of a tailspin with the next thing Amenhotep was about to say.

He came over and placed his hand on my shoulder, and He asked, "How would You like to retire from being a shutterbug? At least, as a livelihood, I mean?"

"Okay, enough with the riddles and innuendo, Amenhotep. My

mind can only take so much," I scolded him. "First, You're leaving Me, and You will be informing Me to where You are heading to, by the way. Then you're telling Me that you're giving Me the Palace, with the stroke of a pen, like I was flesh and blood, and even turning over control of the remaining service slaves in the house to Me. You have to know this is really overwhelming to hear, especially without proper warning first? What makes You think I am ready to bear all this weight right now?"

Amenhotep maintained His grin, expecting me to have this exact reaction.

I hate it when He did that shit. "I wouldn't put all this on You if You weren't ready for it, youngster. You're like a son to Me, and it's time that I actually put some effort behind those words. Besides, this is the next level of Your awakening. It is time that You embraced it."

"Okay, then give Me all of it, everything. I have a wife and kids to tell all this to, and they will have to adjust to this as well. Make sure that You leave nothing out, either," I advised.

I had a feeling this was going to be a long conversation…one that would change my life as a Dominant forever.

☥

Into everyone's life, a little rain must fall…

But was this really rain?

Driving home from work, my mind raced with all of the details from Amenhotep's discussion with me: the Palace, which was completely paid for; the service slaves, five in total number, to tend to the house itself; the male submissives who tended to the house were under Neferterri's control now, to coordinate with their respective Dominas; and finally, the burden of letting the Internet and real-time BDSM community know, in the words He carefully crafted, that the change of power in the Atlanta BDSM community would transfer from Him to me.

You want to talk about *pressure?* How do you replace an icon?

But the one thing that literally put the brakes on my whole thought process...and quite literally made my heart skip five beats or so... was the fact that Amenhotep was going to transfer an astronomically huge amount of funding to run the Palace, put my wife and me into early retirement, take care of the kids' college tuitions, regardless of where they attend school, and invest monies into whatever entrepreneurial ventures that we saw fit.

To put it mildly, Amenhotep, for all of His spendthrift ways I had always known, was a multimillionaire several times over. In fact, He took the funds He would need to purchase and move into a quaint five-bedroom beach home in the U.S. Virgin Islands like he was purchasing a new suit or a new purse for paka. I always knew He was more than comfortable financially speaking, but I had no idea it was to this extent.

But what was so unnerving was, after doing so much to make sure we were comfortable on our own, to now realize we could literally do whatever we wanted to do. I honestly didn't know whether to be happy, or let my ego stay pissed off that we couldn't finish the job. In the end, I convinced myself Amenhotep wouldn't do this if He didn't care deeply for us.

Even with the information overload, His last announcement floored me.

I saw it coming, but it was still a shock to the system.

I came through the door with this look on my face that immediately concerned my wife, but she wasn't sure how to place it. To be honest, I wasn't all that sure how to explain to her that life was about to get easier now. Checking on investments; partying at night while the kids were with the nanny or with one of the grandmothers. The list was endless.

"Okay, You told Me You and Amenhotep talked, so, what happened?" Neferterri was not in the mood for the long innuendo. The kids were at my parents' house, so it was easier to let loose the emotions that were pent up inside of me.

"I feel like we hit the lottery, babe," I started. "He's basically given us the keys to the kingdom, to say the least. Money, the Palace, You name it, we have access to it."

I'd never heard my wife scream so loud in my entire life.

"You mean, we get to quit our jobs?!?!?!?!" she asked excitedly. "What in the world has gotten into Amenhotep? Is He going to die or something? Not that I am wishing that on Him or anything, but what brought all this on?"

That's when I got to tell the other part of what had my mind so scrambled. "He and paka are getting married."

She slapped her hand over her mouth to stifle yet another scream. The consummate bachelor, no one would have ever thought Amenhotep would settle down. After all, He was in His late forties, and with no heir to the throne of His own, it would be a little late to start now, unless He'd gone completely batty. "Are You serious?!?!"

"I'm as serious as a heart attack," I replied. "They want us to make arrangements to meet with them as soon as we're able to have the kids taken care of so we can be witnesses. They are going to do this privately. No one else will be viewing this union except a select, trusted few. Those are the terms they want. You know how Amenhotep is, baby. One minute He wants the world to see, the next minute, He wants complete privacy restriction."

"Okay, I need to breathe." Neferterri found the first chair that she could find.

Not like I blamed her. The club was doing well, no doubt, but the grind of actually rotating weekends on top of the regular 9-to-5 was really starting to wear thin, not to mention the whole babysitting thing, even though that had stabilized, thanks to a teenaged daughter of a lifestyle friend of ours. Now, the prospect of actually not needing to coordinate things anymore hit like a ton of bricks. Reality has a way of doing that to you.

I heard the phone ring while we were both trying to compose ourselves, and upon looking at the caller ID, I had a feeling reality was about to drop in again on another accord.

"Hello?" Neferterri answered as she clicked on the speaker for the two of us to hear.

"Mercedes, it's Kitana." Her voice was trembling, and this time it didn't sound like it was from just hearing her voice.

"What's wrong, honey?" Neferterri's ears perked up when she noticed the concerned tone in my voice. .

"It's Ice. He's…he just left me. He wants a divorce."

23 ∞ RAMESSES

Damn.

Just when I thought things were finally beginning to clear up a little bit, Ice goes and gums up the works. Something didn't sit right, and I had to know what the hell actually happened.

Neferterri was on the phone with Kitana, getting the lowdown on what actually set Ice off: as it turned out, Ice took exception to Kitana being our submissive, even though he was submitting to Mistress Sinsual at the same time. He felt since she had me, she didn't need him anymore, so, it was in both of their interests to be with other people and not be with each other anymore. What had me confused was why he felt it was worth saying the words he wanted a divorce from his wife? Did he have a change of heart about his wife being in the lifestyle or something, but he could still do his thing? I couldn't figure it out, and I think I had to figure out what was on my shotgun partner's mind before this union became broken beyond repair.

I finally found him at one of the usual hangout spots out in Decatur, popping shots left and right like he was trying to forget about whatever it was that he'd just done. No one was messing with him at the bar, for fear he would snap. That's always been the thing about Ice: once he's pissed, he's not easy to be around because of his temper.

Right then, that was the last thing I was worried about.

"Yo, Ice, talk to me, dawg," I started. What I saw coming to greet me was an unexpected left hook that caught me flush across my cheek, knocking my glasses off my face. I forgot how hard he could hit someone, and I ended up trying to catch my balance against a chair while the whole bar got quiet.

"What the fuck do you want, Kane?" I could tell Ice was in no mood to talk, because he was coming at me again with malice in his heart. I braced myself against what could've been coming next, because I honestly had not come to start a fight. "You got what you wanted; what the fuck do you need me for anymore, huh?"

"What the hell are you talking about, kid?" I responded, trying to block the punches as they were coming at me. I finally got hold of him to get him to talk. "This is me, Kane; what is wrong with you?!?!"

"I'll tell you what's wrong with me, dude." Ice broke loose from my grip and sat on a bar stool. "I made a decision, and my wife didn't want to run with the idea. I wanted her to drop her commitment to you and be with me and Mistress, so we could submit to one and one only, and she refused. Right now, you're my fucking problem."

He was actually pissed!

I stood there in disbelief at my friend. We'd been boys since college, been through some pretty fucked-up situations in our time together, and some pretty damn good times as well. Hell, Kitana had chosen him over me back in the day, and now he wanted to play it out like I was the problem? To divorce your wife over something this petty just felt wrong as hell to me.

"Ice, what has your Mistress said to you? I've been your boy for damn near ten years. We go way back...what the hell is creeping in your mind, dawg?" I wanted him to level with me, because something wasn't adding up. He owed me that much, especially when it felt like our friendship was about to come to a screeching halt.

He still wouldn't answer me, so I unfortunately had to do something I really felt like I was going to regret afterward. I pulled him by the back of his collar, dragged him outside to his bike, and basically commanded him to inform me of his Mistress' words to him. I didn't want to pull the D/s card out in public view, but it did the trick. His eyes got big when he saw that side of me. It was a surreal moment for me, too.

He leaned against his bike, shoulders slumped, eyes on the ground, like he didn't have the strength to look at me, and he replied, "Mistress wants Kitana and me both, Sir. She feels like it will complete Her House as well, and She wanted me to convince my wife to leave Your consideration and submit to Her at my side, saying it will strengthen our bond to each other to submit to Her together."

I sat on my bike, speechless. Here I was, thinking I was being greedy about trying to keep Kitana and Angel within my House, and Sin was pulling her own power play to take Kitana away from me?

I shook my head and sort of laughed to myself. Yes, Sin was a friend, but all's fair in love and submissives. Had it been anyone else, I would've probably pulled her card and called her out in the community for breaking protocol. But I would have to deal with her later on tonight.

Poor Ice. He was stuck in a really bad position. Because he feared his Mistress more than his wife, he may very well have ruined his marriage.

Damn. How does a person get over that obstacle? Even if they were able to talk about this, knowing this revelation may really cause a rift between them, over some silliness based upon a Domina's ego. The weirdest part was that Sin had a sub girl already, and I know She hadn't released her because she had been loaned out to another Dom a couple weeks ago for training. It didn't sound like Her, though. She, like most Dominas, had submissives of both genders coming at Her left and right.

This was messy. But I owed it to my partner to help him straighten this out. He'd do it for me. I knew it.

I grabbed him by the shoulders and made him look up at me. "I'll square your Mistress, bruh. This was not your fault, and She knows She should be ashamed of herself for putting you in this position, if what you say is true," I told him, trying to get him to release the stress in his mind and on his heart. He loves Kitana, this I knew. No one had the effect on him that she did, not even his newfound Mistress.

"Thanks, K. I'm sorry about the punches, dawg. We've been through too much to let it come down like this." Ice apologized, his demeanor changing to the positive with each passing word. "What about Kitana? I really fucked up, man."

"Kitana loves you, dawg. Never doubt that. It'll take more than a misunderstanding to break you two down."

24 RAMESSES

On the way to Sinsual's house, I kept cycling the conversation with Ice in my head over and over again, making sure I hadn't missed a single detail, anything that would lead me away from what really didn't make any sense. Mistress Sinsual has been a part of the inner circle for damn near a decade. She's been honorable in every sense of the word, and where she might have slipped, she's made amends for the transgression. The dots weren't connecting right, and I hated the doubt in my mind at that moment.

Who do you trust?

I drove past the Cascade Road exit, and it would only be a matter of time before I got out to where Sin lived in Mableton, so I needed to get my mind right and clear when I got there. There was no need in being indecisive at all. Ice was my partner in crime, a brother of the flesh. But I had to be honest with myself: would I have trusted another male submissive to make such claims against a respected Domina within the local community?

I called my wife to let her know what caused Ice's meltdown and he wanted to apologize and talk to Kitana while she was there. She said she understood and she would make sure Kitana and Ice would patch things up, even if she had to make Ice suffer for a day or two. I couldn't argue the point because he could have sought out counsel on this before he had that confrontation so he could think things through. Sometimes it caused a problem for a new submissive to want to please their Dominant so badly they abandon all logic.

There'd always been this fine line when it came to dealing with submissives for me. If they'd pretty much been upfront with me on a consistent basis, I would respectfully go to bat for them. But if there was cause for me to think I may compromise my own honor because said submissive withheld some vital information from me? Then said submissive would go down in flames quickly. I made sure to try to stick to my mantra for as long as I'd been a Dominant. It was what Amenhotep has taught me, what my father taught me before I began my journey within this realm.

I pulled into Sin's subdivision, and already I felt my body heat beginning to rise. That always happened before I had to interrogate anyone, especially one so close to the inner circle. I got out of the truck and walked to her front door, wondering if tiger was at home or not. It was nearly seven in the evening, so he could be there, but then again, it wouldn't matter much anyway. I told Sin over the phone that we needed to speak, Dominant to Dominant.

Sin was a very striking woman, about Amenhotep's age, in her late forties. I'll admit my libidinous side had been lusting after her for a long time, but I knew she's not the socially sexual type. Now, if there was space and opportunity, of course, I would have to make a call to my wife to inform her of what may transpire, just as an FYI. Those wanton feelings aside, I have always respected Sinsual and our longer conversations about our respective pasts as well as our shared passion for protocol. Which was why the accusations Ice levied were so confusing to me.

Sin opened the door for me, and after trading the usual long hug, she led me into the living room and offered the chair for me to sit in while she stretched out on the couch. She could tell I was struggling with what I wanted to discuss with her, and to be honest, I was.

I cut to the chase, rather than beat around the bush; I owed her that much. "We've been friends a long time, Sin, so be real with Me," I hoped she would want to be civil in person to figure out why she felt the need to want to undercut me. "Did You suggest to Your other submissive under consideration, Ice, that Kitana needed to be with You?"

Sinsual gave me this look like I had lost my mind. When I explained the events with Ice and Kitana, as well as the incident at the bar earlier, it finally started to take shape in her head.

"That boy," was all she could say as she shook her head. "he's worse than what tiger was when I was breaking him in. Always too eager, and never listens."

I raised an eyebrow. "You mean You didn't tell him to convince his wife to leave our consideration?"

Sinsual's expression turned rather embarrassed. "I wondered out loud during one of his training sessions if it would be better if his wife were alongside of him, since she was doing so well in her training with You. Your friend is quite the hardheaded little son of a bitch."

I laughed hard on that statement. He was hardheaded during initiations into the Knights, too, so it was sounding more and more like a submissive trying to stay out of more trouble by creating little white lies to keep it from getting back to his Mistress.

Still, I had to be sure to check this out, face to face. It has often happened that Dominants will try to sneak a submissive away from the touch of the one they are already under consideration of or collared to. Sometimes one has to face that type of situation head-on; otherwise it could be seen as weak in the minds of fellow Dominants in the community. Even if it was a friend, no one should be above reproach, not even me and my Beloved. Sure, we try to live honorably in the realm as Dominants, but every one of us makes a mistake or two in their journey.

Sinsual shook her head at me. "I know You had to do what needed to be done, Ramesses, as I would have probably done the same of You. These days, it's been more and more difficult to trust anyone in the community. All these newbies coming online and not caring about the rules of engagement, protocol, all that we hold dear in the realm." She didn't have to speak to that at all. It's what a lot of the veterans had been frustrated with for the past several years, and what kept those like Amenhotep from even taking the risk of going online.

"Yeah, I know what You mean, m'Lady," I replied. "If it weren't for some of the swingers we know who are curious about expanding into BDSM, I'd be hard pressed to find a female submissive nowadays."

"This reminds Me, m'Lord. I have a submissive who has approached Me who wants to serve a Domina. Do You think Neferterri would be interested? he is a bit new, but he has served a Domina before, albeit for a short time," Sinsual asked me.

Now, this presented quite the unique circumstance. For years, there had been many who had wanted to serve at the feet of Lady Neferterri, mainly because the male subs do talk. A lot of them have all stated to un-owned male subs that would listen that they would be honored to serve her if they were not already serving their current Dominas, and do quite enjoy when they are loaned out for her use and abuse. But like most Dominas, Neferterri was very particular about the submissives she chose to serve her, and they usually don't last very long, once they realize the service does not require long sexual sessions. Imagine that?

But there was also the other dynamic, between myself and said sub male. In the past, the sub males who presented themselves to her, also wanted to serve me as well, but they had a sexual agenda to go along with that servitude. With me being heterosexual, that simply was out of the question. In the grand scheme of things, I had to make sure I was not causing a monopoly over what subs can and cannot be acquired by the House.

"Send the information to Her, m'Lady. I'm sure She will be interested in what You might be sending Her way."

25 & RAMESSES

I made a quick phone call over to Ice and Kitana's house while driving home from Sinsual's to make sure things were okay between them and that Kitana understood the reason why her husband acted so irrationally. Her voice changed, sounding like she was a teenager talking to her crush while she was on the phone with me.

What was it about submissives when they heard their Dominant's voice?

Once she was reassured her husband never had any intentions of divorcing her, I turned the attention to her next visit with us, and continuing the next phase of her protocol training.

I got through the door, and after checking on the kids to make sure they hadn't torn up their playroom, I finally found my wife on the IMs, doing the usual juggling act between a few people.

"Hey, babe, I just got off the phone with Kitana. It seems that things are back to normal, so to speak, at their house," I told her, trying to read over her shoulder to make sense of the conversations she was having.

"Hey baby, how is Sinsual doing?" my wife asked me as I quickly kissed her on the cheek. She seemed to be in a better mood after the situation I'd put her in earlier, and I quickly began to see why that was the case.

I saw an unfamiliar screen name on the screen, and from the way it seemed, whoever it was, they had captured Neferterri's attention for longer than five minutes.

lady_neferterri: *Hello.... Mistress Sinsual sent Me your name*

by_her_command: *Good day Ma'am*

lady_neferterri: *how are you?*

by_her_command: *Hello, Dear Goddess, how may I be of service to You today?*

lady_neferterri: *Are you new to this lifestyle?*

by_her_command: *Yes Ma'am, I am very new to the lifestyle*

lady_neferterri: *so what made you interested in this or started your quest so to say?*

by_her_command: *Well Ma'am, I have always been the Dominant in command throughout my career and during my last marriage. I have always dreamed of being dominated and kneeling at the feet of a Goddess that I can respect and serve her in every aspect of her pleasure.*

lady_neferterri: *how old are you? What is your vanilla name as well*

by_her_command: *I am 26 Ma'am, and my name is Damian, Ma'am*

A youngster…

New to the lifestyle, and he had managed to keep Neferterri from going off on him.

This might be interesting after all. Sinsual didn't waste any time getting the info to her.

I continued to read the conversation as it happened, secretly wondering if he would slip up and say something off-color, or perhaps do what the other submissive males tended to always do before it was time: talk about sex.

lady_neferterri: *so do you know anyone in the BDSM community here in Atlanta?*

by_her_command: *Yes Ma'am I do*

lady_neferterri: *good*

lady_neferterri: *do you have any questions for Me?*

by_her_command: *No problem Ma'am, a question I have is what are You looking for in a submissive?*

lady_neferterri: *first...honesty and trust*

lady_neferterri: *must be compatible in that you don't have to like everything I like but have a willingness to be open about new things*

lady_neferterri: *be independent...I'm not looking for a slave...I want a submissive*

by_her_command: *May I ask another question Ma'am?*

lady_neferterri: *go ahead*

by_her_command: *I am new to this and I have been claimed before, however, it didn't work out because I realized the Domina was more about Herself than She was for me as Her sub. How would You treat Your sub on respect for his well-being and enjoyment of serving You? Are You a caring Domina of Your sub, or does caring about Your sub's pleasure to serve You even a concern?*

lady_neferterri: *very good questions*

Very good questions, indeed, I thought to myself. Neferterri looked over her shoulder at me with this grin on her face.

"How the hell Sin decided to give this one up, I'll never know. She giggled at the thought, especially when she knew how much trouble Sin had been going through with Ice. "But I'm not going to look a gift sub male in the mouth and say I don't want him."

"Good, because if Sin did find out She gave up a diamond in the rough, She'd be pissed at Herself," I quipped. "Now, are You going to answer the youngster properly or not?"

She playfully slapped at me as she continued her conversation with him.

lady_neferterri: *My sub's well-being is a major concern for Me. How a sub is feeling, worried, mad, or whatever is going on in their life concerns Me. A sub cannot serve well if things going on in their lives are affecting them or they need their limits pushed.*

by_her_command: *That is wonderful Ma'am*

lady_neferterri: *Dom/mes who go by protocol have to care about their subs. When You take on a sub, their life goes along with it.*

by_her_command: *I agree with You so much. I have met so many people in this lifestyle that haven't come to terms with that. They think it's all about them.*

lady_neferterri: *those are selfish Dom/mes*

by_her_command: *I agree Ma'am, but that seems to be all I have met since getting into this lifestyle*

lady_neferterri: *it's hard to weed out the real Doms from the bad ones*

lady_neferterri: *just like it's hard with finding subs*

by_her_command: *I agree Ma'am. I hate to say it, but subs need to interview the Dominants/Mistresses just the same.*

lady_neferterri: *yeah I don't expect it any other way*

lady_neferterri: *I expect you to go asking about Me...*

by_her_command: *May I ask You another question Dear Goddess?*

lady_neferterri: *yes*

lady_neferterri: *you are free to talk*

by_her_command: *Do You attend any munches or meet and greets in the city? Also, did You have any interest in the DomCon convention this weekend?*

lady_neferterri: *yes and no....it depends on schedule... We have three kids, so got to worry about babysitting*

by_her_command: *Very understandable Ma'am*

by_her_command: *May I ask Your age?*

lady_neferterri: *35*

by_her_command: *Thank You Ma'am. And how does Your husband feel about You having a male submissive?*

lady_neferterri: *if I were to consider you, you would serve Me, but you will obey the Lord of this House as well. you are a submissive, and whether Dom or Domina, that should be expected, once they have earned your trust, don't you agree?*

I loved it when she was able to get her point across.

But then again, considering all of the BDSM chat groups that we participated in where various topics came up on a weekly basis anyway, it didn't surprise me that some of the conversation finally rubbed off. There was always the question of dealing with a Dominant Couple and the dynamics of "Does the submissive *have* to obey the other Dominant within the House?" I don't know about other folks, but there are two, and both will be obeyed. There was no room for anything else to happen.

Neferterri ended the IM conversation with the young man whose vanilla name she found out in the conversation was Damian. She had this half smile on her face as she looked up at me to figure out the expression on my face. To be honest, I actually was pleasantly surprised. Trying to find a decent male submissive of color was probably more difficult than finding a female.

"So, do I get to keep him, Daddy?" she asked sarcastically.

"You got jokes today. He must have impressed You to go through all that," I replied.

"Yeah, he has so far. But I'm going to see how he reacts once the conversation turns sexual." I knew what she meant by that. Even the ones who could put up a good front in terms of not talking about sexual topics until a certain time, all of a sudden become the deviants they were trying to hide once a Dominant's guard was down.

The usual game of cat-and-mouse: regardless of vanilla or alternative lifestyle, the game never faded.

"If things go as You hope they will, yes, we will go through the normal protocol procedures, baby. If we are going to do this, it has to be done right," I finally told her. In actuality, I had already figured that sooner or later, there would be a male submissive within the House. With Amenhotep leaving soon, a lot of things were changing fast, which meant we needed to make sure that we got our House in order quickly, as other things would be holding my attention.

That meant figuring out what to do about both Kitana and Angel. One of them was easy to figure; the other one, I wasn't so sure about yet. I guess it was simply a matter of finding out, one way or the other, and that was what I intended to do.

26 ꙮ RAMESSES

Something didn't feel right.

I noticed things were amiss, making me pause. I paused when I noticed the tone of her voice when she agreed to meet with Neferterri and me at a bar in Midtown, not too far from where she worked. My wife felt the uncertainty in me, which echoed her own suspicions as to why Angel didn't want to meet up at a more public venue, and not on an off-day.

There's something to be said for someone who does things on such an undercover mode. What's done in the dark, I think was what the old saying goes. To be honest, it made me question something else she might have been hiding: the nature of her relationship status.

There were a few things I mentally omitted from my mind when we were having sex after Neferterri turned Angel over to me: insisting on doing it doggy style the entire time we were sexing; not wanting to perform orally, which is a big turn-off for me; and not getting dressed fast enough when her cell phone rang before we finally got done because "it was getting late and she needed to get home." For a woman with no kids who worked as an exotic dancer, that seemed a bit strange. Hindsight was 20/20, and it made things painfully clear to the both of us: Angel's leading a double life.

I pulled into the parking lot of the bar where she wanted to meet, and I immediately wanted to turn around and drive home. The place was a hole-in-the-wall, the type of place where you take someone you didn't want the general public to view for any reason. Not well lit, which said a lot considering it was still mid-afternoon. Everything about it screamed security nightmare, and it simply put Angel in a very unflattering light.

Neferterri saw Angel walking out of the bar and heading toward another car, never seeing us while she was strolling. I began to do a double-take because of the make and color of the car she walked toward. It was the same as the one outside of the house a few weeks ago. I almost wanted to get out of the car to confront him right then and there, but I remembered my wife was in the car, and Angel was standing there with him. That wouldn't have been the smart move to make.

Neferterri felt my tension. "What is it, baby?"

"That's the car I saw outside the house," I flatly answered. "I know that's the car. I remember the wheels."

She tensed up. "Do we need to leave now, before something goes down, baby?"

I understood her wanting to leave, and I couldn't blame her. I was actually glad we took the "POS" car, so to speak. Whenever I felt the need to be inconspicuous, I drove an old-style Ford Crown Victoria with tinted windows. It disguised itself as an unmarked police cruiser, which works beautifully when I don't want to be noticed. Don't ask me why I did it, but I didn't want to take any chances.

Yeah, I know, but I'm a cop's kid.

Our suspicions were realized when a familiar figure popped out of the car to embrace Angel: Lee, the jackass who didn't recognize my wife when he decided to call her out of her name that night at the club, was standing in a trench coat with a collared shirt and pants.

"Well, I'll be damned." I sat there in mild shock. No wonder she had to get home so quickly. He must have been waiting at home for her or something and wasn't appreciating having to wait when he called her cell that night.

"Baby, let's go. We got all we need to get right now, Angel's history in My eyes," Neferterri told me, obviously irked over seeing all this in person. "The fact that she's even with this dude is making My stomach turn."

I was inclined to agree with her, especially when I had sex with her. Slowly but surely, I began to find things wrong with Angel, things I was willing to overlook before. Damn, why all the fine ones got to have issues? But my wife was right. There was no need to even drop this chick in person; it's better to let sleeping dogs lie. Besides, I had better fish to fry now.

As much as my wife was ready to split the scene, I wasn't quite ready to leave. I needed to make sure before I called my friend at the precinct.

"Give Me five more minutes, honey. I need the plates just to be sure." The guy was smart to back the car into a corner; I'll give him that credit. But Lee had to leave sometime, and I wanted to nail him to the wall to figure out what the hell he wanted with me and mine.

I got my wish about a couple of minutes later, when Lee's cell phone went off and when he answered it, he rushed Angel out of the way and got in his car. He sped off quickly, but not fast enough for me to confirm the plates my father's friend had given me on the partial plates I had.

"Bingo," I said before starting the engine.

"Okay, Shaft, now can we go?" my wife impatiently asked, sounding irked at my wannabe cop routine.

"Yes, we're gone. I need to turn this over to the authorities so they can follow up on it." There was no way I was going to try and handle this myself. I'm not a cop, nor did I want to be. But I'd be damned if I was gonna sit by and let some nut try and disturb the peace that is my home and family.

Now the question was did I want to know the answers to the questions in my mind?

☥

"We're being followed."

There was a car that took up a surveillance position almost as soon as we left the bar.

"Are you sure, baby?"

"Yes."

Maroon color. Chevy Impala. Twenty-four-inch rims. Not the smartest idea on the planet to tail a person in such a conspicuous vehicle. That let me know that his crew wasn't all that smart, especially when they were casing the house a couple of weeks ago. Not smart at all.

I had to keep my calm so I didn't freak my wife out too much. But I had to put some skills to work a little bit. So, without warning, I made a quick right down Sidney Marcus, put a few cars between us for a minute, enough so I could see them and not tip them off. I made a left on Piedmont with the intent of popping in a circle in the middle of Buckhead to see if I was correct.

Damn.

As soon as we hit Piedmont, the Impala followed. This couldn'tve been happening.

I slowed the pace a little bit, letting the Impala play catch-up for a minute. I needed to see the faces of our pursuers. I recognized the two guys from the incident at Liquid when Lee had popped off at the mouth and almost caught a beat down.

We were approaching I-75 South, so I smoothly made the transition down the two-lane stretch of road where the interstate exit merges off and the rest of the stretch of road heads toward Spring Street.

Before they could figure out what I was doing, I jerked the car onto the exit merge going to the interstate, leaving them no choice but to head toward Spring Street. It was too late to merge with the rest of traffic to catch up with us.

Neferterri looked at me like she'd never seen me before. "Where is my husband, and when the hell did he learn to drive like that?"

I laughed it off, as some things were not always needed until the moment arises. Those skills were taught long before I'd married my Beloved, back when I was a youngster being groomed to be a State Trooper like my father before me.

Some habits never die. I'm glad this one hadn't left me.

My wife grabbed her phone and dialed Angel's number. I felt the anger on her as she waited for the voicemail to pick up.

"You are no longer being considered as a submissive of this House, Angel. Your actions have proven you untrustworthy and unfit to be a submissive of Kemet-Ka. We wish you peace in your journey, and make sure that you do not darken our doorstep again."

"Well, that was one less issue to concern ourselves with." I laughed. "Now, we only have the Halloween party to deal with after we go through trick-or-treat hell and we'll be home-free."

27 ⊗ NEFERTERRI

Coming through the door as instructed by the email she'd received from me earlier in the day, Kitana had no idea of what to expect. It was her first time coming through the front door in submissive mode, and her mind raced. She made sure to memorize the instructions that Ramesses and I had drilled into her over the last few weeks. Now, on the verge of Amenhotep's departure and pending nuptials, it was time to showcase Kitana to see if the circle of friends would be pleased at her progression or not.

The guest list was quite large, considering the way that word spread about Amenhotep and paka's soon-to-be departure. But then again, it's not entirely surprising that most people would want to see the two of them off. Sinsual and Blaze were in attendance with their bois, which meant Ice would be in attendance as well, to see the emergence of his wife as a submissive. I was curious to see how he would react to seeing her in a D/s atmosphere, and it looked like I was going to get my wish.

Out of the corner of my eye, I watched Kitana snap out of her trance and crawl into the grand room, where she made sure to quickly locate me, since I was the closest one to her. She immediately took her place at my feet at the end of the sectional couch, assumed her kneeling position, and kept her eyes cast downward until I acknowledged her presence. I saw Ramesses looking on, smiling at the entrance Kitana had made, and capturing the attention of every Dominant in the room.

"Good girl, and on your first night, your Sir and I are pleased," I said. Kitana then began to hear the other comments from the other Dominants that were in the room.

"Very nice; she learns very quickly," I heard Sin say to the audience, while stroking tiger's head.

"she will make an excellent pet, Sir," one of the other Dominants, Lord Magnus, commented to Ramesses, shaking his hand. "I see that the House of Kemet-Ka is still alive and well, Ramesses."

"You say she is brand-new to the community, Neferterri My; she is quite a find indeed," Blaze stated next. "she resembles shamise in so many ways, I am pleased she has found her way into your House, Neferterri."

Kitana blushed and grinned to herself at the impression she made. Above all else, she wanted to make Ramesses and me proud of her, and she managed to accomplish that in front of a captive audience.

"Yes, she is, and we are very pleased and proud of how much she has absorbed in the short time she has been with us." Kitana finally heard Ramesses's voice, barely containing herself. I softly pulled her hair to keep her mindful of her feelings.

She felt his hand across her shoulder, and she tried to keep from shaking. His presence always had a way of commanding attention, and not because of his height. Ramesses made sure he commanded respect and attention without saying a word.

Kitana's relationship with me was just as intense, but in a different way. While Ramesses had the blessed ability to control her mind, I had begun to develop the exquisite ability to take her body to new levels of ecstasy. In her mind, it was the perfect combination, and she felt herself lucky to have found her new House.

"you may look up now, Kitana, so we may introduce everyone to you." Ramesses took his finger to raise her face toward his.

Kitana finally had her first opportunity to see who was in the room. She was surprised to see about three other Dominants and two more Dominas, along with about six submissives, both men and women, at their places of ownership at their owners' feet, in addition to Sin and Blaze, tiger and Ice, and Amenhotep and paka. It was quite a sight for her as it was the first time Kitana had seen other male submissives before. The male subs don't come out a lot, including her husband, who was not far from her in his kneeling position.

Kitana noticed one of the male submissives staring at her lustfully, and remembered she was still naked. While it turned her on to know she attracted attention, it was the way his eyes fixated on her that made her uncomfortable in her stance. She also didn't like the look Ice gave her as he noticed the looks she got from the submissive.

I spoke sternly to him, letting him know of my displeasure. "Did I give you permission to fix your eyes upon My property, slave?"

"No, Ma'am. Please forgive me, she is so beautiful, Ma'am." He cast his eyes to the ground immediately, not daring to speak any more than he had to.

"That's no excuse, slave, and you know better than to disrespect your Mistress."

Blaze overheard her submissive being berated for his transgression and immediately took her hand and raked it across the back of his head, dropping his head down and forcing his eyes shut. "Just for that, slave, you go back into your chastity belt."

"Yes, Ma'am, as You command," he replied sheepishly as he settled back into his kneeling position.

I calmed Kitana down and told her, "Do not hesitate to inform

Me or Daddy if someone looks at you in a way you are not comfortable with, little one. If you haven't figured it out already, your Sir is very protective of you, My sweetness."

Sin was stroking Ice as she took notice of a sickening sweet smile that spread across my face. Her curiosity got the best of her when she asked, "So, what is on Your mind, Neferterri? You look like the cat that just swallowed the canary."

The answer to her question came in the form of my surprise for the evening, which was the submissive male I had been chatting with for the past couple of weeks, Damian. He immediately located me and couldn't stop smiling as he slowly walked toward me.

I noticed something in the way Damian walked as he approached me that caused my mind to click a little bit, and it made me smile even more at the additional possibilities now opened to me to do to him. It was something I needed to bring out of him, to get him to embrace and feel comfortable with this revelation, and get my Beloved comfortable...well, maybe not Beloved, as he's dealt with this situation before and it didn't bother him then, so I knew it wouldn't bother him then.

The other Dominas in the room fell silent as he walked. A couple of them couldn't take their eyes off him, considering he was nearly as tall as Ramesses. I tried to keep my composure, too, but my mind drifted back to the first meeting we'd had. You could slice the sexual tension with a knife, and I had to keep from raping him then. Seeing him again, in the jeans and muscle shirt I required, was enough to send me over the edge.

He made his stop at the base of my feet, dropping to his knees with his head bowed, stating, "Good evening, my Goddess, please forgive me for my tardiness. How may i be of service to You?"

I wanted to say something, but my ability to speak was delayed by the lust in my heart. I knew I wasn't supposed to, but I had so many thoughts I didn't know where to start.

Blaze fanned herself. "Good Lord, this boi right here…"

Sin, realizing she had handed Damian over to me on a silver platter without at least meeting him first, drooled over the sight of what she could do nothing more than play with…with my permission, of course.

Even Kitana couldn't avoid staring at him, which was giving me even more of an ego boost. It was safe to say I made a very good choice. I lifted his chin to meet my gaze and replied, "No worries about being late, pet. In fact, I think the ladies were quite pleased by the surprise appearance, I would say."

Looking around the room, Damian noticed, as Kitana before, all of the people in attendance fixated on him, including Ramesses and Amenhotep, who grinned and shook their heads at the spectacle in front of them. Unfazed, I caressed his cheek and commanded him to kneel at my other side, opposite Kitana.

"Remind Me to kill You for not telling Me I gave up such an exquisite piece of a submissive," Sin whispered into my ear. I giggled because she was right. I would have told her in a heartbeat if Damian didn't meet the standard.

"We do need to talk about a co-Topping situation if he acts right, Sin," I calmed her down quickly. After all, we were closer than sisters, and I wouldn't trust anyone else in that type of situation anyway. "Right now, he seems to be going okay, but I have to put him through some nonsexual atmospheres to make sure he's as real as he is putting himself out to be."

"I can understand that, Neferterri, because something that fine has got to have something wrong with him, just to balance things out a bit," Sinsual replied, still drooling a little bit. I looked down at tiger, and I know he had to be a little jealous of what his Domina was doing to him. "Besides, you haven't taken My tiger and scened with him in a while, and I'm sure he's been a good enough boi to deserve a scene with his second favorite Domina; haven't you, tiger?"

tiger tried hard to keep his grin to himself, but he couldn't contain himself. He looked up at Sin and silently asked permission to speak, and upon her nod, he sheepishly said, "Yes, Ma'am, it has been a while. i didn't want to appear wanton for a scene with you, Ma'am, so i wanted to be patient until Mistress felt i deserved the opportunity."

I guess it was my time to shine, and I was glowing big-time tonight.

"I believe it is time to retire into the basement; don't You think, Ramesses?" Amenhotep asked, knowing it would be interesting to see this new audience react to the changes Ramesses had made to the Palace. "I'm sure the guests are ready to head into the bewitching hour."

"Yes, Sir, let's do this," I heard my husband say, giving me a wink as he turned to head to the basement.

He had been over here off and on for about two weeks, making the adjustments to the Palace as he saw fit, without a word of opposition from Amenhotep, and the basement was the final touch, so to speak, that would make the Palace completely ours.

I couldn't wait to see how the new dungeon looked…and boy was everyone, including me, in for a surprise.

28 ∞ NEFERTERRI

The basement of the Palace was transformed into another world.

The St. Andrews Cross, actually there were three in total now, were securely fastened against the far walls, in their own spaces. There were also a few work benches, in the middle of the basement floor, suitable in their separate locations: to have a willing, or unwilling, submissive become the center of attention should the occasion call for it for the one bench in the middle of the floor.

On the other corner of the basement, the fire cages were already lit, with a complete set of tea candles on each cage. Next to the cages, a "suspension swing" set had been fastened against the corner, for anyone that might be tempted to get into any suspension torture.

Ramesses had had the ceiling reinforced with steel beams as well for anyone that might want to suspend their submissive or slave in mid-air. The new additions to the dungeon: the display stage, also in the center of the basement, not far from where the spanking benches were located; a built-in shower for water play and shower shows; a designated location for fire play and electro-stimulation, complete with a fire extinguisher.

Next to the fire play area was an extensive "First Aid" closet that was the size of most bedrooms. There were speakers in every nook and corner of the basement as well, to give a surround sound capability when scene music would be played.

When Ramesses wants to put *his* mark on something…

Kitana looked against the wall near one of the Crosses and saw the wide array of floggers, whips, cat-o-nine tails and riding crops hung neatly on the hooks, as was the case at the other Crosses. She was in awe of the pleasure and pain each piece potentially possessed, and her body shivered at the thought of what might happen to her this evening.

Before Kitana could get any closer to the toys to admire them more, Ramesses commanded, "We have guests, little one. Take your place so you may witness before participating."

She hid her disappointment as well as she could, but I could see it in her face. She wanted to prove to Ramesses she was ready to handle whatever was thrown at her. Kitana took her place at her Sir's feet, leaning her head against his thigh as he took her hair and began running his fingers through it.

I noticed Ice's face as he saw his wife being fawned over by her Dominant. He was going to have to get over it. After all, Sin usually did the same thing with him as well, and usually openly, as Ramesses did with any of the girls we had.

"Be patient, Kitana. you will get your turn soon. I promise." Ramesses caressed her as he said it, reading her body language.

"Yes, my Lord," she softly replied, enjoying the feeling of him caressing her hair. They were seated near the Cross in the center of the dungeon, at a vantage point where they could see everything without much obstruction. "i can't wait to suffer at Your hands, my Lord."

She heard light slapping noises coming from the area of the Cross. Kitana looked up and saw I was engaged in a bruising flogging display on the male submissive I'd chastised earlier in the evening, with Damian in his kneeling position, taking in the whole scene.

"Kitana…" I heard Ramesses call out to her.

She couldn't take her eyes off the force my lashes produced. What had her even more mesmerized was the look on the submissive's face; one of sheer pleasure mixed with pain. I felt the heat from her. It turned her on to see me in such an aggressive state. She unconsciously began playing with her nipples, watching me slap harder…and harder…

SMACK!

A stinging pain shot across Kitana's ass, catching her off-guard. She knew Ramesses' hand was the source of the sting, getting her attention in a way only he could. I briefly glanced over, temporarily stopping my scene, watching for her expression of being corrected in public.

"Did you forget where you were, little one?" Ramesses' eyes pierced through her like a hot knife through butter. "What were you doing with My property?"

"i'm sorry, my Lord." she lowered her head shamefully.

"Now, what do you think I should do to you for your mistake?" Ramesses asked.

This was the tone Kitana feared the most, her Sir's anger. It was also something she wasn't quite prepared for. It was the first time she had done anything wrong. Her eyes lowered, and she replied, "You must help me to correct the mistake that i made, and You must punish me in the way that You see fit, my Lord."

She braced for whatever Ramesses would do next. After a brief pause, I heard him say, "I will have to punish you, little one, but not right now. No one saw your transgression but Me, so, nothing has been done to embarrass us."

He gave her a small kiss on the lips to reassure her, led her to where I was, forced her back to her knees, and commanded, "Now, watch what happens when you do not do as you are told."

She watched me, and by this point I had taken the submissive literally by the balls and began to twist and torture and punish him more severely than before. His look no longer was of pleasure. It was now of sheer pain and a slight bit of fear of what I would do to him next. I begged him to use his safe word sadistically, but he refused every time. Finally, he got to the point where he could bear no more and cried out, "*No mas!*"

Blaze, who had been watching the entire time, called him to her side as soon as he was released from the Cross so she could console and talk to him about why he was punished. Kitana also bore witness to this sight, understanding there would be comfort after the punishment.

"Do you understand now, Kitana?" Ramesses asked.

"Yes, my Lord," Kitana answered. In her mind, it was best to watch than to receive, and if she could help it, there was no way she would earn punishment. That was, unless, she wanted to earn a "punishment," so to speak. "May i inquire what we will be doing now, my Lord?"

"you've been a good girl so far, little one." Ramesses stroked her face as he said it. "Now it's time you please us tonight."

29 ⊗ NEFERTERRI

"Remain exactly in the position you are in. Don't move a muscle."

I ran my hands up and down Damian's body, caressing his chest, his stomach, his thighs, his calves, then back up again slowly. I never touched his shaft or his balls, though he longed and almost ached for me to do so. I wasn't about to rush this, even though my body betrayed me in ways I hadn't prepared for.

After a while I focused my attention on his now erect nipples. I allowed my fingertips to tease them, pinched them first, then gradually harder and harder. He groaned, and I noticed he closed his hands into fists.

"You had better not come until I say you can. Do you understand Me?" I said as I caressed his buttocks.

"Yes, Goddess, it is my duty to please You always." He tried to sound calm as the first blow fell.

I spanked him at varying speeds and intensities, settling into a rhythm, increasing the speed and force of the blows, massaging and caressing his muscular buttocks between spanks and squeezing his ever-hardening girth between my fingers. I used my left hand to caress his lower back and the top of his buttocks while I spanked with my right. At times I trailed the nails of my left hand up and down his back, creating an overload of sensations on his body.

Soon we were moaning and breathing heavily as my right hand

made contact again and again. I slowed, wanting to draw our session out as long as possible, loving the delicious anticipation.

I reached underneath to tease the tips of his nipples with the fingertips of my left hand again. My right hand tenderly caressed his nicely warmed buttocks, giving him a few quick sharp spanks on the tender lower halves. He gasped at the increased sensations. I set a steady rhythm, varying the intensity of the blows all over—sometimes caressing, sometimes delivering a blow, causing Damian to cry out while tightening his thighs around his throbbing shaft.

I finally stepped away from him, needing to take a breather and get my increasing heat to calm down. I walked to the wall to get a couple of the suede floggers in anticipation of taking him over the edge. I saw Sinsual in the corner of my eye, using the pinwheels for their delicious intentions on tiger, noticing Ice off to the side in his position, watching and waiting for his turn.

I was high, craving my new sub boi. I stifled moans as the wetness trickled down my thighs as I watched his body slowly move back and forth while still cuffed to the Cross.

Damn, I thought to myself, *was this how Ramesses felt when He was with the girls?*

I took my time returning to Damian, stalking him, using the floggers in my hand as new-found weapons in a mini-war I already knew I was winning. Unfortunately, by the time I had finally gotten back to his naked form, the war I waged against my body to hold out for its own pleasure was completely lost.

Knowing my husband like I did, I knew he had a private room built in the basement, same as was the case in our own home. I scanned quickly until I saw a door near one of the Crosses, out of the way of the crowds, perfect for a clandestine escape into bliss.

I unhooked Damian from the Cross he was on, dropping him to his knees immediately upon release from his cuffs.

"Come with me, pet," I commanded, keeping him on all fours as we headed to the room.

The private room was big enough to accommodate about four or five people, set up the same way as the room in our basement. On the four walls, candelabras were affixed, meant to be the only lighting in the room. The bed, king-sized for maximum usage, was placed and bolted to the floor in the center of the room. No windows. Colors draped in our House colors of Royal Blue and Purple. The soft feel of plush carpeting beneath our feet completed the ambiance of the room, and we noticed a door to an accompanying bathroom to clean and freshen up before leaving to join the audience in the dungeon. It was quite the simple splendor indeed.

"Lie down on the bed, pet," I commanded.

"Yes, Goddess," he replied, crawling onto the bed and lying on his back.

I straddled his face first, and he reached up and pulled my hips down to him, eagerly licking my dripping lips. I took my hands and began stroking his length, getting him hard enough so I could get a condom on him when the time came. I knew I couldn't hold out too much longer if he found a rhythm with his tongue. Sure enough, he found my most sensitive spot and began flicking his tongue across it.

I rested my full weight on Damian's face, grinding into his tongue as I came for the first time tonight, gasping and crying out as my body shook. With the condom on already, I lifted from his face and straddled him, taking him in a single thrust and riding him hard and fast. He met my thrusts with fervent reciprocity, moaning and crying out as my muscles worked their magic.

"May i come, Goddess, please?" I heard him groaning, trying to stave off his pending eruption.

"Not yet, sexy...hold on a little longer," I leaned down and whispered in his ear, clamping my lips tightly around his swollen member. Looking into his eyes, I saw his desperate need to release, and I felt my own orgasm coming on hard. It was just a matter of time before I succumbed to the wave flowing mercilessly through my body.

Damian requested a second time to come, but by then my own wave returned. I bucked harder on top of him, trying to ride the orgasm for all its worth. I rode him harder and faster, working my hips against his as the orgasm coursed through me with a vengeance. He held on for dear life, hoping he would get to release soon before he passed out.

When the request for release came the third time, I knew by the urgency in his voice he was at the breaking point. "*Yes, now... baby...now!*"

His body tightened and he wanted more than anything to drive himself as deeply as possible. I matched each stroke perfectly, my thighs wrapped around his hips, leaning so close my lips brushed his ear as I whispered, urging him on. "Yes, that's it...give it to Me. Don't hold back."

Like he had a choice?

In a rush, the wave swept through him, leaving him entirely spent.

I stroked his head and quietly told him, "I need you to clean up, pet. We still have guests we need to attend to."

30 NEFERTERRI

Watching Ramesses with Kitana on the Cross was a thing of beauty.

I loved watching him when he put on a spectacle, showing off for the crowd, using the floggers, paddles, pinwheels against her buttocks and legs, and then swapping her over onto her back to use the smaller floggers to perform genital torture on her clit and nipples, changing over finally to the weighted nipple clamps and pinwheels to whip her into a sexual frenzy.

Kitana loved every minute of it, getting wetter by the minute knowing all eyes were on her, her pleasure and pain, the satisfaction she knew Ramesses derived from it. Feeling the heat of the scene was a new experience for her; having all the different sensations assault her body was something she amazingly welcomed, almost unabashed in her movements.

"I think it's time you two finished things and finally made her Yours, Daddy," I whispered in his ear as he decided between the pinwheels and the knives to use on Kitana next. "I'll go get something special for her while You're in the room."

I got up from my seat and walked to find Amenhotep, who was near the exhibition stage watching two of His girls perform a wax play scene for His entertainment.

"Sir, Ramesses and I are breaking in our newest little one formally. Would You do us the honor of keeping watch until we have finished?" I asked Him as He stroked paka.

"Certainly, My dear," He answered without hesitation. "Enjoy her thoroughly, although I have a feeling Your Beloved is doing that already."

I took a vat of the wax the girls weren't using for their wax play and commanded Damian to carry it to the bedroom. Upon entering, we saw Ramesses was already involved in Kitana, who was on her knees pleasuring him orally while he sat on the edge of the bed.

I whispered into Damian's ear, "Assume your kneeling position and watch; understood, pet?"

"Yes, Goddess, i understand." He quietly obeyed, dropping to his knees and holding the vat close until I removed it from his arms.

This was the moment Kitana craved all night, having Ramesses's thickness in her mouth after so much anticipation and so many erotic dreams. She felt the need to come at that exact moment. Having him towering over her as she kneeled before him was just icing on the cake.

I took my place in a chair near Damian to enjoy the scene as it began to unfold. I got wet again. I had a fetish for watching another woman take Ramesses orally, and I had to restrain myself to keep from wanting to get a closer look.

Kitana looked up at Ramesses, only to have his piercing stare searching the very depths of her soul. His fingers harshly pinched her nipples as his gaze intensified, pushing her deeper into her submissive stasis. Kitana couldn't break free from the gaze, like she was being possessed by his will, and she would do anything for him at that precise moment.

"Worship My dick, bitch," Ramesses's voice deepened as he commanded. "you've wanted this for a long time, My little one. Now it is time to fulfill your dreams."

Kitana let a wide smile escape as she pulled out her Sir's shaft, already fully erect. This was the side of him she wanted to experience: the hardcore, cold and unyielding side to him. She lavishly planted kisses along his length, her tongue eliciting a series of low growls from Ramesses. She felt his hands move from her nipples to the back of her head, forcefully moving her mouth to the head, letting her know without saying a word he was ready for her to put her oral skills to good use.

She wanted to come the moment he slid his full length inside her mouth. Kitana wasn't sure she could take him all, but that wasn't going to stop her from trying. She almost gagged, but she slowed herself from the excitement to control the reflex, and was able to deep throat him with more ease than before.

"Mmmm, yes, Kitana, take it all," Ramesses directed, thrusting his hips toward her mouth with more vigor now. "That's it, baby. Work your tongue…like that, sexy…"

She could tell by the grip on her hair he was close to climax. She quickened her motion, wanting him to explode in her mouth so badly she could already taste it.

Suddenly, the rush she'd waited for all night had finally arrived as Kitana heard a loud growl escape from his lips. The force of his eruption was intense as she made sure not to spill a single drop, and wait for his orgasm to subside. Surprisingly, he didn't get soft. He was still hard, even after coming as hard as he did. "Bend over, bitch; it's time for Me to feel you now."

Kitana turned around and presented herself, wet pussy and ass, for her Sir to appreciate and penetrate.

"I'm impressed you still have on your heels, even at this late hour." She heard Ramesses comment. She was thankful he couldn't see the big smile on her face, even though I could. Kitana always felt sexy and whorish when she wore her heels, mainly because she didn't get to wear them often, but she had a feeling that was about to change.

"Does this please You, my Lord?" Kitana asked with a provocative lilt to her voice. His energy consumed her, enhancing her wantonness with each passing moment.

The answer came in the form of her ass being penetrated first. Kitana squirmed to adjust to Ramesses' girth again, as he slowly slid his full length inside her. It had been a month since they had last been together, but the sensation for her was indescribable as she rotated her hips to get a better grip on his girth.

"Yes, you feel good, Kitana," Ramesses exhaled as he grabbed her hips and began to stroke her anally; taking his time with her until he felt her adjust to him. "Get used to both of us fucking you back here. If you're a good girl, we may have something special planned for you soon."

Kitana might have heard him, but the pleasure from the anal stroking had her zoning out to just enjoy the feeling. "Yes, Daddy, may i have it deeper, please?" she asked, instinctively letting the "Daddy" part slip out of her mouth for the first time.

Her wish was granted, with Ramesses changing her position so he could pull her hair to make the session more intense for them both. I honestly don't think he heard her call him Daddy at that point, but it wasn't as if he really cared if she did or not. After all, this was the culmination of months of work, and this was her reward. He grew more aggressive by the minute, spanking her ass between strokes, the sounds vibrating off the walls. Kitana's moans became more primal, begging Ramesses to fuck her harder. It was almost euphoric, until another surprise came out of nowhere.

Kitana felt slight stinging sensations across her ass cheeks and her lower back. They didn't hurt, but they were distinctly different from the sensations of the friction from her Sir slipping in and out of her. She didn't realize I had gotten up from my spot and taken the vat of hot wax and begun to drip the wax over her back from varying heights.

My voice appeared in her ear, reassuring her. "Don't worry, little one; it's only wax. Just enjoy."

She was already at the point of no return, slowly slipping deeper into subspace with each stroke. The feeling of the melted wax being dripped on her while being fucked anally was more than her body could take. It wasn't long before the wave claimed her body, causing every muscle to tighten.

"Oh, God, i want to come, Daddy…please, can i come?!?!!?!" she shouted out, still taking the steady pounding from Ramesses.

He quickened the pace, to the point where the impact could be heard through the door. He finally realized Kitana had been calling him Daddy and it seemed to take him to a new level of aggression. I had taken a spot not too far from them, masturbating as they were in the throes of animalistic lust. I saw Damian getting excited as well, and I was greedy for another explosion myself, so I pointed in his direction for him to crawl to me and take care of my pleasure.

"Make her come hard, baby. I want to hear her scream out Your name when she comes," I screamed out, feeling Damian's tongue hungrily sucking my clit.

He pulled her up close to him by the hair again, this time angrily whispering in her ear, "Whose pussy is this, bitch?"

"*It's Yours, Daddy, it's Yours. Take it, Daddy!!!!*"

"Then come on My dick now, bitch. Make Me want to fuck you some more," he commanded of Kitana.

"*i'm coming, Daddy!!!! Oh, my God, I feel it…harder, Daddy, please!!!*" Her body tensed, and she buried her face into the rug and screamed as wave after wave swept over her unmercifully.

"That's it, Daddy, come on me...come on my ass!" Kitana held on for dear life as Ramesses slammed into her like he was possessed.

Kitana was commanded to flip over on her back and spread her long legs wide and took her fingers and worked herself frantically as she watched Damian sucking my clit and making me come again from watching her being taken so forcefully. She felt the next wave hit quicker than she expected, and she was soon joining me in screaming out as her body shook through the wave, coming close to pulling a multi-orgasmic wave she desperately craved.

Ramesses finally let out one last primal growl before coming all over Kitana's clit and lips, and shot one load onto her stomach. I could have sworn it was the sexiest image I'd ever seen in person.

Ramesses tried his best to quickly gather his composure. He knew he still had guests he needed to attend to. He whispered something into my ear before coming over to Kitana to place a small kiss on her forehead. He gave her a knowing wink before exiting the room.

"Come to Me, Kitana," I commanded, prompting her to crawl over to her and lay her head on my lap next to Damian.

"Yes, my Goddess, what do You command of me?"

"you will assist Me in ensuring the rest of the House is in order once our guests have left. your Daddy will handle the dismissal of the guests Himself," I told her. "We are very pleased with you, little one. We can't wait to finish your protocol training. Forgive My manners, Kitana, I'd like you to meet your potential sub brother, Damian. Damian, this is our newest submissive, Kitana."

I gave them both a kiss on their foreheads, and as Kitana went into the bathroom to freshen up, I got up to put the candelabras out so that we could rejoin the rest of the crowd and put a close to a rather decadent night.

31 ∞ NEFERTERRI

I honestly thought it was safe to enjoy a decent night out.

After coming out of the private area, I ran into a confrontation I didn't expect to find. At the base of the stairs, Ramesses was in an intense discussion with a Dominant I could tell was not thrilled to be in my Beloved's company. But that's nothing new; it's not like we get along with everyone in the community. What caught my attention was the submissive at the Dominant's side.

jamii, our former submissive, stood in the midst of the dungeon, in a heated conversation with Ramesses.

I made my way over, with Kitana and Damian at my sides, to see what the problem might have been.

My Beloved seemed to have his demeanor under control, considering the guests were all around us enjoying the night's festivities. It was this Dominant jamii was with who seemed to be coming unglued.

"Just admit that You weren't man enough to keep this lovely piece satisfied, Ramesses," I overheard him say as I walked up.

Ramesses felt my presence behind him, but that didn't stop him from firing back, "Just admit that this lovely 'piece,' as You describe her, is happy with You, regardless of what she might have told You went down within the House."

"My name is Sir Xavier, Ramesses."

"Then tell me something, Sir Xavier," Ramesses continued. "How long have You known our former?"

"About two months."

"Figures." Ramesses glared at jamii, but Sir Xavier tried to divert his attention back to the source of the tension.

"What the hell does that have to do with the fact that Your sub-collecting ass can't keep all Your subs happy?"

I started to jump in, but Ramesses grabbed my hand. "Relax, Beloved, it's obvious that our former has been a bit upset about the turn of events of the past couple of months, and she felt the need to have a champion for her cause to teach Me a lesson. Is that about right, submissive?"

"my name is now isis, Sir." She really was trying hard to disrespect, even when Ramesses was trying to keep his calm. "i would greatly appreciate it if i were addressed as such, Sir."

"I will address you in whatever manner I see fit, submissive, until you remember your place," Ramesses bellowed loud enough for a few people to hear him. "I do not care who you submit to now, *WE* taught you better than this insubordination you are showing now. Right now, you're acting like a common trick off the street. Do you really want Me to treat you accordingly?"

"You will not treat her as anything I do not allow You to treat her as, Ramesses." Xavier tried to step between Ramesses and isis, thinking his chivalry in defending his lady's honor would endear him to the crowd.

Big mistake…

"Oh, don't worry, Sir, I don't think You could treat her as anything she would allow You to treat her as." Ramesses stared him down, moving into his personal space, challenging him like they were on the street. "Where did You come from anyway; who vouched for you to even be on the grounds?"

"At least I am submitting to a real Dominant..." came flying out of isis' mouth out of the blue. The point of no return had been reached.

The next sound the guests in the basement heard was a loud *THWACK!*

The next thing those who bothered to turn around to witness was a sight that even shocked Amenhotep...and it took *a lot* to shock Amenhotep.

isis was on the ground holding her cheek looking up at a severely irritated Lord Ramesses. He stood over her with a scowl on his face that scared the hell out of me and Kitana.

Sir Xavier looked like he wanted to protect what was his, but one look from Ramesses stopped any ideas that he might have had there. Looking down at isis, he still felt the need to make some attempt at protecting her.

He swung at Ramesses, catching nothing but air. The next two punches belonged to my Beloved, catching Xavier on his jaw and the back of his head, dropping him to the floor face-first.

As much as the crowd tried to remain composed, the *oohs* and *ahhs* rained down on the scene as all play scenes stopped in favor of the drama surrounding the new Lord of the Palace.

Amenhotep stepped forward, staring down at Sir Xavier. He shook His head, wondering for a moment what made Xavier try to take things to the next level.

"You, Sir Xavier, are no longer a welcome guest upon these grounds. You and Your property are free to leave on your own, or I can have security escort you from the premises," I heard Amenhotep say to Xavier amongst the silence. "Understand the events of this evening are of Your doing."

"You mean to tell me that You are going to allow a Dominant to hit a submissive in Your domain, Master Amenhotep?" isis pleaded, still on the ground nursing the bruise on her cheek.

"you are the last person to question Me, woman," Amenhotep scolded. "Or would you like for the rest of the guests in here to know the reality of your disrespect toward the House of Kemet-Ka upon your requested release?"

isis looked up at Sir Xavier, who had a confused look on his face, and then at the throng of guests now making their way toward the commotion. In an instant, the leverage she thought she'd had disappeared.

"What is Amenhotep referring to, isis?" He asked of his submissive.

Ramesses saw the result of the misdirection that had befallen Sir Xavier. The flash of anger in his eyes was evident, and almost like someone had flipped a switch, Ramesses calmed down. He realized the woman Sir Xavier thought he knew was nothing more than an opportunist. The confusion over whether to protect her honor was evident on his face.

"Ladies and gentlemen, I apologize for the interruption in the festivities," he started. "Would anyone like to vouch for Sir Xavier and isis? It seems that they have managed to attend a private affair without the ability to name the persons who claimed them as their guests."

Silence for nearly two full minutes.

"Well, since no one wants to claim these two as guests, then I must ask security to escort them from the premises. Ramesses has spoken." He headed upstairs and out of our line of sight as the security personnel executed his order.

Sir Xavier left his property on the ground like she truly were something he'd picked up last week. isis picked herself off the ground and, without much more word or sound, left the dungeon area after her Dominant, who I suspected no longer wanted to be her Dominant anymore. He'd been embarrassed in front of an entire group of people within the lifestyle who took honor very seriously.

Amenhotep looked at Kitana and me, saw the expressions on our faces, and He calmly spoke. "Do not fear, My dear ladies. Ramesses is fine; He unfortunately had to revert to someone you both may not recognize. Go to Him now; He will need you to balance Him again."

While Amenhotep attended to the guests to calm them down and get them back to the festivities of the evening, I sent Damian to assist Him while Kitana and I searched for Ramesses upstairs. We finally found him in one of the guest bedrooms, trying to regain his composure. He rocked back and forth at the edge of the bed like he wanted to shake something off him.

Kitana immediately fell to her knees at his feet, trying to get him to look at her. I sat on the bed next to him, rubbing his back to let him know what he did, he had to do.

"Daddy...we're not afraid of You, so please don't think that." Kitana stayed on her knees, head bowed, as she talked to him. "she left you no other choice. she was not acting as a submissive should act."

"Our little one is right, baby. We need You here," I told my husband. The only thing we could do was stay with him until he could snap back out of it. As long as we'd been married, been a part of this lifestyle community, Ramesses had never lost his composure. It was a source of pride for him, and he had to be reminded his honor was still intact.

He finally rubbed his hands together, a sign to both of us he was starting to balance out a little. Ramesses finally opened his palms to us, and we each placed a hand in his and watched our hands get swallowed by his long fingers.

I saw Kitana shudder. Hell, I couldn't help it myself. I felt his electricity course through me, and I could tell it affected Kitana as well. It's funny how that works out sometimes.

"Alright…we still have guests to attend to, ladies. Let's make sure they are well taken care of so we can keep our circles intact, shall we?"

Moments later, Ramesses was back to his usual flamboyant self.

32 NEFERTERRI

I awoke the next morning completely refreshed and still high from the night before.

I guess that's what happens when a small fortune has been placed in your lap to control and maintain. Waking up in the Palace as the new owner was still something I wasn't used to, but I had to get used to the idea quick because it was something I had to help promote and maintain. So, I got a pen and paper and began jotting down my "to do" list.

The first things on my mind were tying up some loose ends on a variety of fronts, now that I no longer had to work, per se. So, I called my boss to inform him I would be putting in my notice of resignation. Needless to say, he wasn't entirely thrilled with the idea of his right-hand person leaving him, but I kindly reminded him it was the slow season heading into the new year, and I would be able to have a suitable replacement at his disposal before I left him. I told him I was still working for the next month to ensure my replacement would be up to speed, and the transition would be near seamless.

He kind of relented at my exit strategy, but he was still upset I was leaving him. For the past five years, he had been trying to get with me intimately. He knew I wasn't exactly into white men on a sexual level. Well, that, and I don't mix business with pleasure. If that were the case, I would have sampled every one of the dancers at my club. He was a cutie pie no doubt, just not my cup of tea, so, he unfortunately would not be able to sample this particular dessert before I departed. So, when I flipped through my possible replacements I had been considering, I made sure to find ones I knew would be able to handle the fringe benefits he was willing to give me. Not to mention having the ability to do her job as well as keep her mouth shut about the perks she was getting.

I finally settled on jezzabelle, Blaze's pet. She had the proper credentials to be able to do the job, and the appetite to give my now former boss everything he could handle and then some. A quick call to Blaze to let her know her pet had a new job and a better rate of pay, and it was on to the next thing on my "to do" list, which was taking care of the club.

I called DeAngelo to find out from him if he wanted to buy me out or not. He had this perplexed sound in his voice, like he didn't expect to hear those words come out of my mouth. To be honest, I didn't expect them to come out, either. But right then, I had a different path to follow, and that path was leading to the Palace.

"Are you sure you want to do this, cuz?" he asked me one final time, trying to talk me out of it. "It's not gonna be the same without you, and you know the girls are gonna be pissed they don't have you as a boss anymore."

"Yeah, I know, and I still might change my mind, D. But I'm on the verge of something big, and I know Kane; he's gonna want my undivided attention." I wasn't lying about that. Knowing my husband, he had some big plans, and now that we had the cash flow to get it done, the sky was the limit.

"I hear you, cuz. Tell Big Game I said congrats and I wish you two the best," he replied. "I guess there's nothing left to do now but figure out the dollars to make this buyout work for the both of us. I'm not trying to slight you, and I know you don't want to sound like you're selling yourself short."

I had to admit, I wasn't sure if I was ready to give up my baby just yet. After all, D and I had built her from the ground up, gone through those years in the red, sinking hard-earned money from our full-time jobs, sacrificed what had to be done to get it off the ground to being successful. Now that it was, was I ready to leave? I really wasn't sure about it, which was quickly leaving me quite torn. Could I juggle two businesses at the same time? Could I be the power player I dreamed about being when Kane and I were younger?

"D, wait a minute, I'm not ready yet. I thought I was, but…" I really heard myself hesitating, and it was killing me.

"Talk to your husband about it, cuz," he reassured me. "He might not want you to give up. That is what you're thinking, right?"

I hate it when family knows you so well sometimes.

On the way home from my soon-to-be old employer, I was trying to figure out in my head what conversation I was going to have with my husband. In my heart, I wanted to keep the club. After all, it suited a lot of purposes, including a central location to be able to handle meet-and-greets without having any issues pop up. Not to mention the money the club would generate to open up the possibility of opening other businesses.

My mind tried to rationalize dealing with the kids and how they would handle the transition of Mommy and Daddy working at night, but that argument was BS too because we were already doing the night shift on some weekends anyway, so nothing would really change there. My mother and mother-in-law would be able to help out with the kids anyway, as they had been, except now they could both retire so they could be paid to handle them on a full-time basis. I smiled at that thought. They'd always been active in their upbringing, so this wouldn't change much.

In the end, I pretty much figured out he might have already thought about that as well, and he would be gung-ho with trying to develop more "vanilla" businesses, to be able to diversify our revenue, and at the same time, create some jobs as well.

My cell phone rang. I couldn't see the number because it was privatized, and normally I wouldn't have answered the phone, but I had a feeling I needed to pick it up. Call it woman's intuition, I guess. I felt a slight chill come over me as I answered the phone, and I soon realized the reason why.

"Your husband is going to pay for fucking with me," I distinctly heard Jasmine's voice, but it was definitely more panicky, more stressed. "I just thought you might want to know that before I go inside and have my people drop him like a sack of potatoes. My husband will be taken care of soon. I told you that you were all going to pay."

"*Jasmine? Jasmine!*" I yelled into the phone as Jasmine hung up, but because she hid the number, I had no idea of where she could be, who she had with her, or anything. What's worse, if she had done something to Jay, then I knew she would make good on her threat against my husband.

Damn it, I shouted in my head. *I need to get to Kane now.*

My mind went into panic when I couldn't reach him by cell phone. It really didn't help matters because Jay's phone was rolling straight to voicemail. I had to call Candy; there was no other choice in the matter, and I needed my girl to help me think. The last thing I needed was to get to this point, only to have him taken from me so unfairly.

Once I got through the front door, I tried to keep from pacing the floor. I was trying to figure things out, but all I accomplished was heightened anxiety attacks. Thankfully, the kids were at my mom's house that night, or I'd have really lost it by then. Candy's number popped up on my screen, and I picked it up immediately, rambling on and on to her, not giving her a word in edge-wise.

"Mercedes, calm down," I heard her say over the phone, but I really couldn't hear her completely. My husband was out there, and I had no way of figuring out if something had happened to him. "Where was he supposed to be today?"

I slowed my thought processes down. I needed to think. I went over to the calendar to see what he was supposed to be doing today. I saw *Bank w/Amenhotep* written around the 3 o'clock time slot. It was around 7 p.m. now, and he hadn't called me back or returned any texts I'd left in the last forty-five minutes. It wasn't doing me any good to try and calm down.

"He should have been home by now, Candy. It's not like him to change his routine without calling me to let me know." One thing about my husband: he's always cautious. He didn't take the same way home from work two days in a row. He left work at a different time every day. It's all to keep anyone from trying to track his movements.

"Baby, you need to calm down. He's with Amenhotep; have you tried calling over there to make sure that he's not over there?" Candy asked, showing a little concern in her voice now, realizing maybe I wasn't panicking for nothing.

The house phone started ringing, and I prayed hard it would be Ramesses. Again, the caller ID showed a private number, and I cursed out loud because I didn't know whether to answer it or not. "Hello?"

"He's not at the bank, sweetie, and Amenhotep is a little 'tied up' at the moment." Jasmine's voice came through as cold as an arctic breeze. "He's okay, for now, and he will stay that way until you bring your pretty little ass over to my house. Oh, and don't forget my darling ex-husband. After all, it is only fair. You helped take my husband away from me, so I might have to return the favor."

The phone went dead, and I went completely numb.

"Mercedes, talk to me," I heard Candy yelling through my cell phone. "*Mercedes!*"

I put the phone to my ear finally and told her what I had just heard. "She's got Kane."

33 ⊗ RAMESSES

My head throbbed.

My senses slowly came back to me, but the intense pain from the blow I took to the back of my head was nothing nice, to say the least. As each one began to surface, my mind took inventory of what exactly was happening to me. The last thing I remembered, I was with Amenhotep leaving the bank, and then I saw Jasmine waving frantically at us like she was in trouble.

A sharp pain scorched across the back of my head, then another across the right side of my jaw.

Then darkness consumed me.

I couldn't tell if it was night or not, but it had to be because we'd left the bank just after closing time, around six.

Amenhotep…

The first thing on my mind concerned my mentor. If I had been unconscious, what had become of Him? Had He been harmed and kidnapped as well…or even worse?

It didn't take long to figure out Jasmine had played us, and now the question in my mind was exactly who had helped her kidnap me? I'm not a small man by any stretch of the imagination, so even if she had gotten help, it would have taken at least two others to drag me to wherever the hell I was.

My arms were bound behind me with rope, ankles tied down to

the legs of the chair, and my wrists were expertly secured to the arms of the chair as well.

My eyes were open, but I only saw the dark fabric that bound my eyes to shield me from whoever was in the room with me. I could taste fabric against my tongue, and the distinct salty taste of my own blood within the texture of the fabric in my mouth. I guess someone decided to take some target practice while I was out, either that or I hit the ground pretty hard after being hit.

My hearing became hypersensitive, taking notice of running water to my left, and voices trying to whisper in conversation with one another. I knew I wasn't alone, but I wanted to know how many people I needed to blaze through to get out of this mess. But who was I kidding? I didn't have a gun on me, and you can't win a gunfight with your bare hands.

"He's not so tough now." A male's voice I heard.

I could recognize the voice: Lee. *Son of a bitch...*

"Don't get cocky, he's wasn't easy to bring down. You found that out when you had to hit him a couple times." The other male voice in the room I couldn't make out, and I could hear a faint voice yelling from behind me. That meant the count was three, the number of men who were holding me captive.

But damn, a couple of times? No wonder my head hurt so badly.

I detected a female's scent and her presence entering into the space around me. She started caressing my cheek, which was strange to me. Why would she be treating me like I was her lover?

"Now that I think about it, I should have married you instead of that weak-ass punk friend of yours."

It was Jasmine.

She untied the gag in my mouth, and I felt the cold rush of ice water flowing down my throat immediately afterward. My throat couldn't catch up with the rush and I found myself choking for a minute, but the water kept coming. I felt it sliding down the sides of my mouth, trailing down my chest and shoulders until the water flow finally stopped.

"That's better. I wouldn't want your girls to find out I mistreated their precious Daddy." She laughed as she said it. "The great Ramesses, huh? Not so great now, are you, *my Lord?*"

I was still coughing water out of my mouth, so I really didn't have a snappy comeback in mind. She still had the blindfold over my eyes, so I couldn't really see what expression she had on her face, although I'd imagined she was definitely exulting in my misery right now.

"Exactly…what…are you…trying to prove, Jasmine?" I kept trying to take breaths in between the words that felt hard as hell to say because my throat was so tight.

"That I'm in control, playa," she angrily retorted. I heard her moving across my right side, again stroking my cheek lovingly. "Aww, did my boys bruise that handsome face of yours? I'm sorry about that; that blow to the head was supposed to put you out."

The fingertips I felt caressing my cheek a second ago were now replaced by cold steel. My mind processed the barrel of a .380 stroking my skin now, and for the first time, it was real.

Her intent was to do some major harm if she didn't get her way.

My sense of smell was coming on strong, and I could distinctly pick up cannabis on her breath. That made for a really bad combo, and my anxiety factor kicked up a notch. I made a mental note not to enrage her any more than she already was, but I needed to get her talking so I could figure out how to survive long enough to live through this craziness.

"Let's just do this punk and be gone." I heard Lee yelling, sounding more agitated by the second.

I was dying to have this blindfold taken off, so I could at least face my captors. A man in my position deserved at least that much.

"Why are you...doing this?" I huffed, still trying to control my breathing. The pace was steadying now. I felt my lungs filling without the fire I was experiencing a little while ago. "Damn it, at least let me see who the fuck I'm looking at before I die!"

The answer to that question came in the form of the butt end of the gun connecting with my jaw.

"You arrogant sonofabitch, I would have figured you could have figured this out by now," she raged. "Come on, it doesn't take a dummy to figure out this puzzle."

"Jay." I wrapped it up in one word. "Jay."

"Yes, Jay." The venom was on her breath as she said her ex-husband's name. "You thought you were in control the whole time you were at my house that day, didn't you? Trying to look all calm and shit, like you had shit played out before he even came through the door."

"Jasmine, Jay is his own man. I thought..."

"*You thought?*" I caught a slap across my mouth again with the gun before the blindfold was ripped off my face. I squinted to let my eyes adjust to the lighting.

We were in the living room of a house I did not recognize. Pastel colors on the walls, art deco placed on two sides. No pictures to give me an idea of who the owner of the house was. I could tell from the lack of light against the windows that it was after dark, but I had no idea of the time. No clock in sight.

Lee was in one corner of the room, and the short stocky dude I remembered from that night at Liquid was standing watch by another window in the opposite corner of the room.

I took one look at Jasmine and, as sick as this might sound to say, but *damn*. The way she was rambling on, I'd have thought she would be ragged, disheveled even, with hair all messed up, wild woman personified.

The vision I saw in front of me was the furthest thing from what I imagined.

She looked like she was ready to head to the club after all this was over. Halter-top pant suit, black in color, four-inch pumps, hair impeccably styled, her makeup completely flawless.

If I wasn't in fear for my life before, I was definitely there now. Anyone who took their sweet time to dress to kill while I lay unconscious was a force to be reckoned with.

Dressed to kill...damn, poor choice of words and then some.

"Since you saw fit to ruin my life by taking my husband away, I thought I would do you the honor of returning the favor and taking your life," Jasmine finally told me.

"Okay, this doesn't have to go down like this, Jasmine. You can't be serious," I pleaded, leaning and turning my head toward where I thought she was so my words could be heard. "Call Jay, let me talk to him."

"Oh, I'll do you one better, *Sir;* I'll call your dearly Beloved so she can see how serious I am."

Before I could protest, she secured the towel over my mouth again. I heard silence behind me, but I couldn't see anything because she was still behind me, then I heard the numbers being punched into the phone. The next thing I heard both relieved me in one sense and completely chilled me to the bone in another.

"He's not at the bank, sweetie, and Amenhotep is a little 'tied up' at the moment." Jasmine's voice came through on her end of the conversation. I kept trying to scream through the towel, make any kind of noise to let my wife know that I was still amongst the living. I felt another pair of hands around my neck from behind me, trying to stifle my ability to breathe, closing in tightly.

"Yeah, put this fool out of his misery so we can get this over with." Lee's eyes moved up in the direction of the source of my distress.

With Lee and the stocky dude still in front of me, I could only conclude that it was the third man in this abduction, the tall dude from the club, who was trying to choke the life out of me.

It was only a matter of time before I would pass out, but I was not about to go down without a fight, period. I kept struggling against the ropes on my arms, trying to figure out how to wiggle free to fight against the tall dude, but it wasn't happening.

Jasmine continued her demands over the phone. "He's okay, for now, and he will stay that way until you bring your pretty little ass over to my house. Oh, and don't forget my darling ex-husband. After all, it is only fair. You helped take my husband away from me, so I might just have to return the favor."

That was the last thing I heard before another sharp pain hit me square across the back of my head, covering me in darkness once again.

34 ⊗ NEFERTERRI

God, I can't lose my husband...not like this.

A million thoughts and emotions went through my mind while Candy and I were on the way to get Jay.

Candy tried hard to keep the mood even keeled and tried to talk about other things to keep us both from losing it. Neither of us had ever been in this situation before. The only good news we received was from paka. She told us the police had found Amenhotep and He was a little dehydrated, but no harm had been done. But He was upset to say the least and had begun making phone calls from the officer's phone to locate his former apprentice.

Jay was speechless when I explained what his ex-wife had done. He sat down on the couch with his head in his hands and couldn't stop the tears from flowing. "It's my fault. I never thought she would stoop to such a level. Kidnapping?"

"Look Jay, you might be the only one who can save Kane from her. She's not listening to anyone right now." I pleaded with him, at the same time attempting to keep my own emotions in check. I was beside myself with fear and anger at the same time, but it wasn't Jay's fault. Jasmine had made this choice to go down this path, and there was no way to change it. It was going to end one of two ways: jail or death. I shuddered at the thought, but being a part of a law enforcement family, there was no other way to think.

Candy sat next to Jay and rubbed his shoulders. "I'm with you, Jay. I know this isn't easy for you, but your best friend is in trouble. We need you, baby. Please."

Before we left, I rushed into the office and went through Kane's black book he had hidden in a drawer he didn't think I looked into. It contained information and phone numbers of people he only used for certain "emergencies" that require something outside of police interference. He'd have to kill me later. I was desperate to find out where he was, and the only people who could find him without arousing too much suspicion were at my fingertips.

I found the number I wanted, but before I could dial it, my phone rang again, and my hand shook as I attempted to answer it. It had the same private call message on the ID, and I tried to garner the strength to answer.

Something came over Jay. Without warning, he walked over to me, snatched the phone away from me and answered it harshly. "You could have left our friends out of this, Jasmine."

I could only hear one end of the conversation, but it was clear there was a power struggle going on as well. "Jasmine, Kane didn't hurt you...look, you need to listen...I don't think so, you've hurt enough people...look, where are you, and don't bullshit me, Jasmine...okay, I'll be there in ten minutes, alone."

He hung up the phone, and when he looked up, Jay saw two rather shocked faces staring at him. It was clear we hadn't seen this side of him before, but then it clicked inside of me as to how he and Kane were when they were both single, and I began to slowly realize I had Jay pegged wrong. I think we both did, considering the look on Candy's face as well.

"I've got to go, ladies. She has got to be stopped before she really does hurt Kane," Jay said, kissing Candy softly across her lips. "I want you both to go to Amenhotep's house. You're going to need some people around you after this all goes down."

Jay knew his shotgun partner would do the same for him, and he had to resolve this, once and for all.

But by then, I was already on the phone with Dominic, asking him for a favor since he was off-duty. I explained what had happened to my husband, my voice trembling with each word that came out of my mouth. I told him I didn't need the police involved, I'd called a couple of the other ruffnecks Kane had always used in the past whenever something needed to be handled off the record. He might have had a clue that I knew about the book, and while I wasn't naïve, I kept out of the madness when I needed to stay out of it.

Upon hearing me finish my tearful rant, Dom let me know he'd ensure that nothing happened to Ramesses. "He'll be cool, sweetness. Tell Jay that we'll meet up with him at his house in twenty minutes, and to stall until we get there," he told me. "In the meantime, go and see if your friend Amenhotep is okay. I just heard on the scanners that they found him tied up near where they kidnapped Kane."

35 ⊗ RAMESSES

All I heard were gunshots…sirens and gunshots.

Everything felt so surreal. I could have sworn that I saw Jay and Dominic fighting with Lee and the stocky dude. The tall dude was nowhere to be found, no matter how hard I tried to twist to find him.

I thought I saw Jasmine on the floor, bleeding from her chest, struggling to breathe…

Feeling the carpet against the left side of my face, I prayed that through all the gunfire, no one had been killed. Someone had been shot. I felt a pain in my shoulder that proved that much, and watching Jasmine not a couple of feet away from me bleeding out, reality was going to be a bitch when I finally became lucid.

My eyes were still glassy, but I thought I saw ghosts drop Lee and the stocky dude where they stood with kill shots.

Ghosts that probably were figments of my imagination. At least, that's what they were supposed to be until they were needed.

The officers finally broke through the door, guns drawn as I saw the ghosts disappear. They immediately started securing the place, a couple of officers helping me out of the chair and the rope I was tied in. I heard police radios going off, asking for EMTs to be brought in to see about the wounded, possibly dead on scene.

As I was brought to my feet and helped out of the door, I took a quick look around the room, taking count of the dead bodies on the floor, swearing my mind was playing cruel tricks on me. Maybe I was hallucinating because I'd been treated like a Whack-a-Mole all night.

The scary thing was…I had a funny feeling this was not a hallucination.

36 NEFERTERRI

Patience is supposed to bring good luck...please let that be true tonight.

Waiting on phone calls while at Amenhotep's from anyone to give us a lifeline to figure out what happened to Ramesses and Jay was absolutely excruciating. I couldn't stop pacing the floor, stopping abruptly whenever any phone rang within earshot of me. Candy was as I had never seen her in a long time: agitated and at a loss as to what to do. She had always been the rock for me whenever Ramesses had to go somewhere with his father and he couldn't tell me the specifics, but now the shoe was on the other foot and we had to lean on each other. It had been a couple of hours since Jay split from us, and the silence was killing us all.

Amenhotep worked every back channel at His disposal, and even He was finding it difficult to get any information. I saw the worry on His face. He's *never* been this nervous before, or at least He's never shown it in front of any of us. paka tried to settle Him down, but it wasn't working. Thankfully, He was in one piece when the police arrived. He had a good knot on the back of His head, and He was a little pissed off the assailants had gotten the drop on them both. He told us there were four of them, three men and a woman, and they came out of nowhere while they were on the way back to the car. He knew it was Jasmine because, according to Him, she wanted Him to know it was her before he was knocked out.

I thought I would have heard from Dominic by then on word of the location. I wasn't going to go down there, I wouldn't be any good to anyone, but I at least needed my mind calmed to know they were able to find my husband. The whole ordeal was driving me insane. I kept his mother and my mother updated to keep the girls calm because they knew one of us would have picked them up from their grandmother's by then. His mother made sure to tell them that "Daddy was with Uncle Amen taking care of some last-minute business." Knowing those three, they would treat it as a sleepover night and not give a second thought about it. In their minds, their daddy was bulletproof.

I hoped at least on this night they were proven right.

Finally, Amenhotep's cell phone rang, and He picked it up before the first tone could finish. "Yes? Okay, we'll check it out." He then exhaled before walking to the big screen to turn to the local news. "I think we're all going to have to sit and watch this. I understand things didn't turn out as the officers had planned."

Officers? I uttered under my breath. *Police weren't supposed to be involved. Dominic promised me that there wouldn't be.*

I didn't know whether to scream or faint, Amenhotep's words were so chilling. He turned on the television, and we saw a house somewhere in Tyrone, which wasn't far from where we lived. I read the ticker at the bottom of the screen:

"Hostage standoff ends in fatalities..."

I kept screaming, *Oh my God*, in my head over and over again, praying for once they would get to the heart of the story quick and not try to build suspense. As the female reporter on scene began to recount what had happened, I could see in the background paramedics were treating both Ramesses and Jay, with Dominic in tactical gear nearby checking on them. I distinctly saw blood on both of them. I didn't see any sign of the other guys who were supposed to be with Dominic, but I guess I should've figured I wouldn't. They had to be ghosts for a reason, especially considering cops were brought in after the fact.

"Be calm, ladies, the contact who called Me said they are fine, just flesh wounds from what I understand. But it doesn't sound good for the young lady and the others that were involved," Amenhotep stated flatly.

As He said that, we saw four gurneys being rolled out in front of the cameras, and then they quickly panned to the police spokesperson to get further details of the incident and confirmed what Amenhotep was saying: four people dead, two officers and the hostage shot in the gunfire exchange. Three males, one female were dead on the scene, with more details to follow.

I felt this uneasiness come over me. Yes, this nightmare was over and my husband was in one piece. But they had been through an ordeal, to say the least. And Jasmine…my God, poor Jasmine… and whoever the other people were were now dead because of a severe bloodlust for revenge. I didn't know how to feel. I kept my eyes fixated to the screen until the broadcast was over, keeping my eyes on my husband the entire time, just to make sure that I wasn't dreaming or my eyes weren't playing tricks on me.

My twilight zone moment finally came to a halt when I saw Dom's cell phone number finally appear on my cell phone screen. I swear it was the best thing I could have seen all night.

"I'm okay, baby. I'm okay," I heard him say over and over on the other end.

"I know…now."

37 ® NEFERTERRI

Time stood still until I got to the hospital.

It didn't take long to find the boys at Piedmont Fayette Medical. By the time we got there, my husband pretty much looked close to his old self. I saw he was still a little shaken up, as was Jay, probably because it's not every day you watch people die in front of you. They were both joking while Ramesses was being attended to. That was his defense mechanism, one that he picked up from his father. Jay was really focused on staying cool for the most part. I understood, because I don't know what I would have done if someone I cared about died in the manner that Jasmine did.

Dominic was filling out paperwork with the nurses and flirting with them at the same time. I laughed to myself, shaking my head. They'd survived a gunfight an hour ago and the only thing he could think of was the lovely young nurse fawning over the "big, strong officer." He finally saw the two of us and motioned for us to head into the room, turning his attention back to the nurse, who wrote down her number as ordered.

Candy didn't know whether to hug Jay or slap him silly. She really was never good at these types of situations. The closer we got to them, the more she shed tears of relief and joy they were both okay, and the "bytch" I was used to finally succumbed to being a woman relieved to seeing her man in one piece.

"You scared the hell out of us both, damn it. Do you realize you could've died? Do you hear me, Jay?" Candy scolded before giving him the tightest hug that I'd ever seen her give *any* man. She turned her attention to Ramesses. "Kane, are you okay?"

Ramesses lifted up in the bed and patted the spot next to him for me to sit. "I feel like shit for letting myself get jacked like that. This was not the way I thought this was going to go down."

Dom walked in and replied jokingly to Ramesses' statement, "That's what you get for choosing to be a shutterbug and not a detective, knucklehead. Not my fault your instincts are getting rusty."

Ramesses laughed off the chide and began to explain he and Amenhotep were in the bank when he saw Jasmine waving at them like she was in trouble and needed their help. When he approached her as they were walking toward his car, she couldn't stop crying, which kept him distracted long enough for three of her thugs to take the back of a gun to his head, knocking him cold.

That was consistent with what Amenhotep explained when we were at his house.

When he woke out of it, he could only hear Jasmine around him, and he was tied down completely with no chance of getting loose.

"She kept mocking me," he said.

At first, Jasmine wanted to have him call me, for dramatic effect, but then she realized I knew his patterns better than anyone. Once she realized I hadn't heard from him, her threats would be taken more seriously. He heard her end of one of the conversations she'd had with us, but he couldn't say anything because she'd gagged him with a towel to keep him from trying to warn us of where he was. Of course it didn't stop him from trying to scream as loud as he could each time she was on the phone.

Jasmine had popped him with the gun again until he'd blacked out. The next time he woke up, Jay was on the ground, face-down with a gun to his head and he heard the faint noise of sirens in the background. By then his head was throbbing and he could feel blood dripping off his forehead. The sirens got louder, and there were distinct noises of the police officers loading weapons.

After that, Dominic took over and gave his account of things from that point, because he had just gotten into the house.

"Things took off quick," he said.

Lee and the stocky dude broke out the windows in the front of the house while the tall dude took a spot in the back. Dom said the guys I called to help out only identified themselves as "J-Roc and Boney-T," names Ramesses recognized as Dominic continued his account.

"J-Roc took out one of the guys in the back of the house and gave me cover while we cleared the rooms, in case there were more than we originally thought," he recalled. "Boney-T popped the third guy that was in another room. No guns, he just manhandled the guy and damn near twisted his head off his shoulders."

Ramesses was still holding the ice pack on his head as Dominic kept rattling off the details. "Jasmine answered her cell phone and talked to the police negotiator to find out what they could do to diffuse the situation. While she was on the phone, Jay saw us trying to make a move on Lee and got up from his spot on the floor. I guess Lee forgot to bind his hands and feet before the cops showed up. Jay lunged at where Lee was posted up at the window. Lee fired a shot off, which triggered the shots from Boney-T and J-Roc. But Lee didn't hit the target he intended to hit."

"What are you talking about, D? Jay took a bullet in the shoulder," Ramesses pointed out.

"You were already on the floor, K. Remember?" Dom pointed out to him. "And Jay never got hit, either."

"He's right, Kane. You must be imagining things," Jay added.

Dominic calmly reminded Ramesses he'd tipped Ramesses' chair to avoid the gunfire coming from Lee's random firing. Lee tried to fire off another shot, but then realized who he hit with the first bullet: Jasmine.

Lee began freaking out as he watched Jasmine bleeding from the wound she suffered in her chest, which tipped the officers at the front door that he was distracted, and they came in blazing. Lee got hit several times in the chest. Jasmine was still on the floor struggling to breathe, and Jay rushed to her side to try and keep her breathing. She died before the paramedics could rush in to administer CPR to get her stabilized.

"The negotiator said she sounded like she was hopped up on drugs, but he wasn't sure," Jay finally chimed in. "She looked so wild-eyed when I came through the door. It was like she'd never seen me before in her life. I couldn't reason with her. She just kept saying, 'I want my husband back,' over and over again."

"I'm just glad you're both safe." I finally opened my mouth. I couldn't stop staring at my husband. It was like we were dating again. "Amenhotep will be pleased that you're in one piece."

"Yeah, thank God He wasn't harmed in all this craziness." Ramesses breathed deeply. "This wasn't His fight. I'm glad He was with you both to help keep things calm."

Candy asked the one question I guess no one wanted to ask. "What happened to J-Roc and Boney-T? Neither of you mentioned what happened to them."

Ramesses gave a look at Dominic, who stayed tight-lipped and stone-faced. He closed his eyes for a minute and said to Candy, "You're on a need-to-know basis, babe, and right now, you don't need to know. Trust me on this one."

In the past, I would have been pissed off at that damn statement.

Now I knew exactly why he said it. Some things we didn't need to know about, as long as it didn't come back to haunt us. I guess my husband was right: J-Roc and Boney-T are ghosts for a reason, and that reason needed to stay with those who could keep those reasons from hitting the streets.

"Well, I don't know about you guys, but I don't want to be in this hospital any longer than the rest of you. Can we head home so we can relax and put this whole nightmare behind us?" Ramesses looked at Dominic again, nodding in his direction. "Do you think you could get that pretty little nurse to page the doctor so I can go? I really would like to go home tonight, if possible."

38 ∞ EPILOGUE

Being on the white sand beaches in Dubai in late November was something out of a fairy tale.

Amenhotep spared no expense to fly a small wedding party which consisted of Sinsual and both of her sub bois, which meant Ice was with her; Myself, Neferterri and Kitana; Master Altar and his slave girl chastity; finally, Lord Magnus and his slave girl jewel as well. Come to find out, Magnus is an ordained minister, albeit retired from actually leading a church, but he also fits as the perfect divine facilitator for this most auspicious of occasions.

He put us all up in suites at the Burj Al Arab Hotel for the week, and arranged for all of us to have separate chauffeur-driven SUVs to make sure that we took in all the sights. Of course, the girls all wanted to go shopping and such, which was fine. It wasn't like we would actually be able to come back there without saving up some serious change not only to stay for a few days, but to sightsee and other things. So, they went to the Al Khaleej Shopping Center, the Al Shindagha Market, the Wafi Mall complex and a few other places, which meant for the majority of the husbands and Dominants in the group, that some credit card statements were going to be rather thick the next month.

I'd never seen my Mentor so relaxed, so at peace, in my life. He sipped on drinks with the rest of the Dominants and enjoyed the luxuries of being in one of the most beautiful places on Earth. Yeah sure, it's my opinion, but I would challenge anyone to find another one without going to a tropical island climate. Every time that he looked at me, he gave me this knowing glance, as if I eventually would be in his shoes one day. I could only hope. But with all the money that he was shelling out for this wedding and festivities, I couldn't help but wonder how much Amenhotep was *actually* worth.

I couldn't help but be overwhelmed by the events of the past few weeks. I had turned my business over to my apprentice, who was more than ready; I'd just been holding him back out of selfishness. For all intents and purposes, "inheriting" a fortune from my Mentor and Father figure to do with as I saw fit, as long as I oversaw his American business interests as well as start a few enterprises of my own. Finally, dealing with the pain and scariness of nearly losing my life and watching someone who was once so close to me, die so senselessly. But it gave me a different perspective on things as well. It was not like I was taking my life for granted to begin with, but I had to be conscious of what reckless decisions can lead to as well. I still have to grow old and see my grandchildren, and live long enough to reminisce on these times that we were living in now.

The night before the wedding, we all sat down as friends for an informal dinner, to enjoy one another more than anything else. No titles. No protocol. And it was good. Amenhotep got a chance to express his love for his soon-to-be wife in a way that re-enforced the bonds that a lot of the other married couples could appreciate and embrace. My wife never looked more radiant, and Kitana never looked more priceless as our submissive princess.

So much so, that I felt that a change was in order.

Once the dinner was over, we went back to our suite, so that we could tell our little one of the news of her new name. Neferterri and I had been discussing it for about a month, since her training had been going along so smoothly and surprisingly quickly. She'd only been ours for a few weeks shy of four months now, but it felt proper to take things up a notch.

Kitana was speechless. She had been waiting patiently for the name change, having submitted the names that she had wanted to be referred by, but also knowing that it would be our ultimate decision. Upon hearing that she would be kneeling for the final time under her old name and rising with her new name, the tears of joy that slowly flowed were the most beautiful things that I had ever seen. It proved to us that she was ready to take the next step.

So, it gave us delicious pleasure to have her rise from her knees to complete her awakening and be recognized as sajira, which is Egyptian, meaning "little one."

We also informed her that upon the first of the year, only a few weeks away, that we would celebrate her new transformation with a lavish, public collaring ceremony. It would be the perfect way to christen the new and improved Palace, which would be undergoing some expansion and modifications from what my Mentor originally had planned. After all, He did want me to put my mark on the place, since it's now to be under my watch. While we were in Dubai, I'd received an unexpected phone call that further made it a magical occasion for the House of Kemet-Ka. When I informed my Beloved of what had transpired, she couldn't stop smiling, either.

The next morning was to be spent in the company of God and friends as the two became one for as long as they both shall live. The groom, wearing a cream-colored tuxedo, nearly blended into the sand upon which he stood. The bride, beaming in an ivory halter dress considering the heat of the Persian Gulf, was draped in rubies from head to toe. The sun was close to its apex in the sky, and the party was dressed in crimson and black, as the couple had requested. Sealed with a kiss, the union would forever be recognized, and the audience applauded at the completion of the ceremony.

It was a wondrous day indeed...one that would not soon be forgotten.

And yet...it was only the beginning.

ABOUT THE AUTHOR

Shakir Rashaan currently lives in suburban Atlanta with his wife and two children. Rashaan's catalog includes the *Chronicles of the Nubian Underworld (The Awakening: Book One, Legacy: Book Two, and Tempest: Book Three)*, *Deviant Intent (OBSESSION, DECEPTION, and RECKONING)*, and a collaborative novel series with Anna J, *Motives*. Other credits include several anthologies, including *Erotic Snapshots Vols. 5 & 6*, *Lies Told in the Bedroom*, and *Zane Presents Z-Rated: Chocolate Flava 3*. You can see more of Rashaan at http://www.shakirrashaan.com.

Visit the author:
Twitter: http://twitter.com/ShakirRashaan
Facebook: http://www.facebook.com/Shakir.Rashaan
Instagram: http://instagram.com/ShakirRashaan
Email: shakir@shakirrashaan.com
Blog: http://blog.shakirrashaan.com

IF YOU ENJOYED "THE AWAKENING," BE SURE TO CHECK OUT

Book II LEGACY
THE CHRONICLES OF THE NUBIAN UNDERWORLD

BY SHAKIR RASHAAN

COMING SOON FROM STREBOR BOOKS

8 RAMESSES

Reagan International Airport, Arlington, Virginia.

I walked off the plane and began making my way down to baggage claim to collect my luggage, and I was already plotting in my head how I was going to deal with the task in front of me.

I walked by the limousine drivers and noticed a rather stacked and stout young lady, about six feet tall, maybe an inch short of that, holding a sign that displayed my full legal name.

I won't trip; I was surprised to see her there to greet me, especially when I hadn't seen her before in my life. But it was a pleasant surprise to be escorted by such a lovely creature indeed.

I guess in hindsight I shouldn't have been too surprised, as I'd suspected that Master Seti would spare no expense in making my stay in the DMV—the DC/Maryland/Virginia area—as pleasant as he could. I'd called the day prior to my departure from Vegas to inform him of my arrival; such is general protocol with any of the Elders that are associated with Amenhotep.

The driver was very attractive. Her distinct features put me in mind of the Italian peninsula. She was dressed in a pencil skirt, just above the knee, and matching blazer, both black in color, and four-inch heels. Her lean, muscular frame left me no doubt that she could handle my luggage with little assistance from me, no matter how much my vanilla chivalry would want to oblige her.

"Good afternoon, m'Lord, this girl's name is slave nadia. Please follow me to the car, Sir," nadia announced as she loaded the bags onto a cart and led me out to the parking lot. "Master has alerted this girl of Your presence, which is why i am driving You to the House, Sir. Master didn't want You lost. He informed this girl that it has been a few years since You've been out this way."

I couldn't help but chuckle at that statement.

"Yes, slave nadia, your Master has a way of reminding Me of such things in the most grandiose fashion possible," I replied as we made it to the Cadillac Escalade Hybrid limousine.

I got in the backseat while nadia placed the luggage in the cargo area to prepare for the ride back to the estate. On the middle console was a USA Today newspaper, and packed in a cooler in the opposite seat from me was an assortment of soft drinks and juices, and a bag of roasted peanuts.

"Master thought that You would like a light snack before Your arrival, m'Lord." nadia read my mind before I could ask.

I couldn't help but smile, though, as this had sajira written all over this one. I would say shamise as well, but there was no telling if she was at the house at the time that nadia called to confirm the items that were sitting on the side of me.

"Remind Me to thank your Master upon our arrival, slave nadia," I responded to her as she slid into the front seat of the car. I noticed a slight blush spread across her face at my statement. That meant she knew that she would be properly spanked for following her Master's protocol to the letter.

We made the trek, beginning from U.S. Route 1 heading toward I-395, passing through the intersecting streets that crisscrossed and made up the Alexandria area. I was taking a sip of the orange juice bottle by the time we crossed over I-395 and continued south heading toward Mount Vernon.

I was reading the paper as we passed by the shopping malls and department stores, going from the commercial into the residential area, when I could feel eyes on me, trying to get a better look at what I was doing. I looked up and saw a gorgeous pair of hazel eyes staring intensely back at me for a moment, before those eyes softened and gave rise to a lust that their owner wanted to act upon, but she wasn't quite sure if she should or not.

nadia was shyly sneaking looks through the rearview mirror as she deftly moved through traffic. She tried to get a peek in right before the fork in the road would either take us to the estate or if we were heading to the Mount Vernon estate, the home of our nation's first president.

We kept this dance up for another half mile or so. Every time I caught her looking up at me, she giggled to herself and focused her eyes on the road again, trying to steal as many glances as she could before we arrived.

I purposely began staring at her through the rearview mirror. The next time that our eyes locked, nadia found her fingers tracing the outline of the blazer. She nimbly lowered the mirror to an angle that I could view, and I saw that during this dance, nadia had unbuttoned her blouse and revealed her bra. I licked my lips at the way the satin caressed her breasts.

She blushed at my open satisfaction at her exposure, keeping one hand on the steering wheel, using her peripheral vision to keep her eye on the road and on me at the same time, and taking her free hand to expose her right nipple for my further enjoyment.

By now, my manhood had made its presence very much aware to me, and I couldn't ignore what it obviously wanted my mouth to say. But this was neither the time nor the place to engage in that type of mischief, as it would be a direct violation of the rules of engagement, and my reasonable half understood that. However, my libido silently crept into the far reaches of where I kept the "Beast" at bay as if to beckon, I have the key to unlock your cage; all you have to do is beg for it.

I wanted her to beg so badly, it made me weak. I imagined her legs wrapped around the small of my back, growling in her ear as I took her in the backseat, the tint in the windows providing the perfect cover in broad daylight before finally getting on with completing the journey.

nadia could sense my dilemma, and I could sense that she was in a bit of a quandary herself. The vehicle slowed for brief interludes, which alerted me to the intimation that she was not yet ready to end this dance.

My intense stare into her now-bright green eyes let her know that I was straddling the thin line between commanding her to pull the vehicle over to the first secreted location for a clandestine and ravenous merging of two bodies and thinking better of it and commanding her to cover herself up before we arrived at the estate.

I shook off the lustful state that I was in as best I could. I had further business to take care of, and I couldn't allow myself to let the "chairman of the board" fuck things up just because it wanted to get wet for twenty minutes.

nadia slowed down long enough to make the turn to the street where the estate was located, stopping the vehicle long enough for the two of us to gather ourselves and for her to straighten her uniform to look presentable once we entered the compound. Once all was back in its place, nadia put the truck back in gear and we headed toward the house once again.

I didn't mind the cat and mouse games too much. In fact, it was a bit refreshing to see such a lovely woman nonverbally flirting without the pretenses of titles and station. Well, at least not entirely. The fact that I am a Dominant in this realm, and a Dominant that nadia had developed a respect for, but she, in the brief time that we'd shared the same space, developed a passion that was predicated upon that respect for my station, and the good things that she had heard from her Master about me.

That was fine by me. It's not like I could not have had nadia hot and bothered under normal circumstances, but at the same time, it helped to not have had to put that litmus test out there.

The next time she looked up at me, I gave a wink that let her know that I wouldn't discuss this little interlude between us with her Master, and blew her a kiss from the backseat to consummate the brief dance between us.

nadia returned the gesture of her own with a kiss in the mirror at me, letting me know that she enjoyed the dance as well, and a wink letting me know that we could continue the dance again, with her Master's permission, whenever I was ready.

Sometimes…it is great to be Pharaoh.

9 ∞ shamise

"What do you mean, you too?"

sajira gave me a look that could have cut through glass.

The look on my face let her know that this was going to be a rather long conversation between sister slaves.

Since we were already finished with the cleaning duties that we were tasked with before Neferterri was due back to the house, we got more comfortable on the sectional so that we could bare souls.

"Okay, sajira, i'm gonna level with you," I began, trying to find the courage to explain myself. "i have been having the same type of rape fantasies that you have been having. i didn't know how to bring it up until you admitted about what your Uber-dom was up to, and, well, here we are."

sajira slid closer to me on the couch, touching my hand as she stared into my eyes, trying to find something that would let her know that this was a cruel joke that I was playing on her.

A few moments later, those same eyes that she was staring into gave her all she needed to know.

"i really didn't know who to tell, sis, honestly," sajira began to confide, her eyes misting. "i eventually want to tell Daddy and Ma'am, but i really wasn't sure what Their reaction would be to it."

Being the more experienced submissive, although I will admit my mindset is more slave-like than submissive now, I felt that my sister submissive needed to be brought up to speed on our Dominants. If anything, it would help settle her mind a little bit, and not be so fearful of them being judgmental. I felt as she did a few years ago, when I finally admitted that I wanted more intense public play, edgier play.

"sis, Daddy and Ma'am do care very deeply for us; you do know that, right?" I asked, waiting for her reply.

I finally got a hesitant nod from sajira, her little girl persona going into full mode. I brought her to me, stroking her hair, feeling her body finally stop trembling.

"The Dominants that we have the pleasure and the honor to submit to have been around for a long time, sis," I quietly told her, still stroking her cheek. "you and i both know that there are few like Them in the community, and i have been in this community longer than you, even though you knew Them from the swing side of things."

"Yes, i know, shamise." sajira nodded. "Every time i'm on the online boards and i sign off with the House name, i get hit up by email from other submissives trying to find out how i'm able to do it."

I couldn't help but laugh at that statement. That question has been around as long as the House has been in existence. Even in poly circles, they just can't figure out how the submissives of the House are able to serve "two Masters."

"That's okay, it's not their business how we do what we do, sajira," I retorted, kissing her cheek. "Just know that as long as you focus on your place and your responsibilities to Them, both as individuals and as a cohesive unit, then you will be fine."

I had this same conversation with jamii and nuru before as well, and it always felt like I had to constantly reassure them of their place in the House, which is how they ended up doing the stupid nonsense that they did in leaving, but this felt different. sajira was already friends of Daddy and Goddess before she made the transition over to the dark side.

I'll admit that it was tiresome to have to do that, and I had no intentions of repeating it again. I like her too much to have her go through those feelings when they weren't necessary.

"Do you want for us to request a free speech, period? we do have that right within the House," I asked her, trying to comfort her a little. The free speech period gives us the opportunity to speak to our Dominants without fear of repercussions or the idea that we're "topping from the bottom.?

"Yes, sis, i would like that very much," she answered, feeling a lot better about things now. "That would definitely help me, especially having you there."

"No problem, sajira," I replied. "Now i need to worry about where i'm going to live, now that i'm back in the city."

sajira perked up on me almost as soon as I finished my pondering aloud. "you are staying with me, no exceptions, at least until you get your own place set up."

My eyebrow rose quickly, which caused sajira to giggle uncontrollably. "i was just saying, sis. you need to be somewhere close to the House, and i want you there with me. What do you say?"

I had to admit, it was a tempting offer, but I had to wonder why she made the offer without talking to her husband. After all, it's his house, too.

"sis, don't you think you need to speak to your husband about taking me in?" I had to ask, as she made the offer too quickly. "Is there something i need to be aware of?"

"Well, shamise, to be honest," she began, her body language definitely changing. "Things at home are tense right now. Ice has changed ever since he began to take his training seriously with his

Mistress. i was thinking that maybe the both of us could help him balance out, because he's not the same man that i married."

I was afraid she was going to say that.

I wasn't sure if I wanted to be in the midst of another power struggle or not. I'd just left one out in L.A. that had left me drained both mentally and physically. Yeah, sure, I had fun while going through it, but once the adrenaline rush was over, it really became a chore to keep up the mess.

But, I did need a place to stay, and being with my sis would be good for us both. It would give us more time together to bond and have a little fun as well. I mean, I am a newly divorced millionaire now.

"Okay, sis, i'll stay with you," I reluctantly accepted her offer. "It should be an interesting time, to say the least."